Praise
DISSEC

'A bracing and beautiful novel...I recommend it as an unputdownable and richly rewarding read, an extended ethical workout of the classiest kind.'
Helen Garner

'[Halloran's] fine analytical intelligence is matched by compelling, rhythmic prose...*Dissection* reads like a moral thriller, a bulletin from the war zone that is modern living.'
Amanda Lohrey, *Monthly*

'From page one, [Halloran's] prose has the unmistakable ring of authenticity...A pleasure to read.'
Dorothy Johnston, *Sydney Morning Herald*

'Hard to put down...Original and thought-provoking.'
Katharine England, *Adelaide Advertiser*

'A tiny gem of a novel...Deeply empathetic.'
Claire Sutherland, *Herald Sun*

'Taut and lean...Beautifully executed.'
Georgia Blain, *Readings Monthly*

ALSO BY JACINTA HALLORAN

Pilgrimage
The Science of Appearances
Resistance

Jacinta Halloran is the author of the novels *Dissection*, shortlisted for the 2007 Victorian Premier's Literary Award for an Unpublished Manuscript; *Pilgrimage*, shortlisted for the 2014 Barbara Jefferis Award; and *The Science of Appearances*. She is a former board member of the Stella Prize, and was a GP for many years.

DISSECTION
JACINTA HALLORAN

TEXT PUBLISHING MELBOURNE AUSTRALIA

The Text Publishing Company acknowledges the Traditional Owners of the country on which we work, the Wurundjeri people of the Kulin Nation, and pays respect to their Elders past and present.

textpublishing.com.au

The Text Publishing Company
Wurundjeri Country, Level 6, Royal Bank Chambers, 287 Collins Street, Melbourne Victoria 3000 Australia

Copyright © Jacinta Halloran, 2008

The moral right of Jacinta Halloran to be identified as the author of this work has been asserted.

All rights reserved. Without limiting the rights under copyright above, no part of this publication shall be reproduced, stored in or introduced into a retrieval system, or transmitted in any form or by any means (electronic, mechanical, photocopying, recording or otherwise), without the prior permission of both the copyright owner and the publisher of this book.

First published by Scribe Publications, 2008
This edition published by The Text Publishing Company, 2023

Cover design by W. H. Chong
Cover image by iStock
Typeset by Scribe Publications

Printed and bound in Australia by Griffin Press, an accredited ISO/NZS 14001:2004 Environmental Management System printer.

ISBN: 9781922790095 (paperback)
ISBN: 9781922791214 (ebook)

A catalogue record for this book is available from the National Library of Australia.

The paper in this book is manufactured only from wood grown in sustainable regrowth forests.

For Michael

With my burned hand I write about the nature of fire.
INGEBORG BACHMANN (AFTER GUSTAVE FLAUBERT)

February 18

Doctor Anna McBride has begun to think of herself first. She has recently developed the habit, if that is what it is, of analysing her own reaction to a patient's story, her feelings about the patient, before anything else. Thinking of herself does not make her feel better: on the contrary, it exhausts and irritates her. But if, in any given situation, she thinks about what is best for *her*, what is the safest course of action for *her* to take, at least, then, she is limiting her exposure. Isn't that what the lawyers would say?

It has become an effort to get to work every day. She has taken to entering through the back door, so as to avoid walking through the waiting room. In the first few months after the writ was served, she continued to use the front door, although, like the physiological conditioning of Pavlov's dog, just the sight of the clinic entrance—the paved stone steps, swept clean of leaves, the small garden bed planted with pink and white petunias—was enough to send her heart pounding. She would be breathless after climbing those four steps and the effort required to push open the heavy wooden door would sometimes cause her to cry with fatigue, as would the realisation that she was not as strong as she had once believed herself to be. She had decided, some months ago, she could not continue entering the surgery like that: tearful and breathless, like some sort of histrionic patient, rushing through the waiting room with her head down, holding back her tears. Such a poor way to start the day. She had initially been ashamed of this decision, seeing it as an acknowledgement of defeat, a backing away from her original stance that everything—her medical practice, her attitude to her work, her life at home—would remain untouched by a negligence claim.

In those first few days, as the writ lay, its manila folder still unopened, in the bottom drawer of her desk, she promised herself that everything would proceed as usual. Why should things change? She had simply made a small error of clinical judgement; an error that, if circumstances had been slightly different, would have amounted to a delay in diagnosis of a week or two. Would have, in essence, all amounted to nothing had the boy, Ben Feltham, attended his follow-up appointment, or had she ordered an X-ray at his subsequent visit. To therefore abandon the front entrance—the bulbous brass doorknob, the white plastic plaque on the adjacent brick wall, bearing her name and qualifications (*MBBS, FRACGP, DRANZCOG*: the acronym proof of her worth) in plain black lettering—might be seen as an admission of many things, as yet unsaid (but that might be said at some time in the future in a courtroom of the County Court); an admission of more than she was prepared, as yet, to yield. But on that first morning, as she unlocked the back gate, climbed the gentle incline of the wheelchair ramp and opened the back door on to a dim and silent corridor, she realised she had already yielded more than was good for her.

Today, on this third Monday in February, she enters the clinic by the back door and, as usual, goes directly to the bathroom to wash her face. In the bathroom mirror, under the dim overhead light, she studies her reflection. What she sees displeases her. Just three years ago, in her fortieth year, she could look in the mirror with, well, not exactly pleasure—there was always room for improvement—but with equanimity at least. The sight of her reflection at forty did not unsettle her, as it does now. The last three years have not been kind. It is not the crow's feet around her eyes, nor the two horizontal creases now permanently etched across her forehead that particularly bother her. Specifics are not her concern. Rather it is the general drawing down of her face, the vertical displacement and slackening of her features, so that now, when seeing herself in a recent photograph, she finds the face that looks back at her both familiar and strange, as if she were studying an old photograph of her mother, or even her grandmother, rediscovered after being hidden for years in some dusty corner of the house. But she does not stand here each morning just to bear witness to her ageing skin. Instead, this bathroom ritual—the washing, drying and scrutinising of her face, reddened from the cold water and the rough cotton weave of the towel—is a therapeutic act, a necessary act of composure before the day's work begins. She no longer knows how she manages it: this piecing together of facial features as she simultaneously pieces together her thoughts, the disparate parts of herself, so that, as she leaves the bathroom and proceeds down the corridor, her fingers trailing the cold brick wall, she presents as the picture of coherence and restraint. How does she manage it? She need not know. Perhaps, like a magician's trick, it is better left unexamined.

The waiting room is almost full. Monday mornings are always busy with the accumulated problems of the weekend. It is, by anyone's standards, a pleasant room to be waiting in: sun-filled and, now, newly carpeted and painted; her share of the refurbishment bill, paid just last week, amounted to one-third of her earnings for the month. A floor-to-ceiling window looks out onto the petunia bed and, beyond that, a slatted timber fence hides the noise and distraction of the street. The children's toys are of an educational kind: wooden puzzles, dominoes in a rectangular box with a smoothly sliding lid, a metal construction set. A selection of recent magazines—*Vogue Living, National Geographic*—are neatly arranged on the large, wooden coffee table. During her training she worked in places with awful waiting rooms, cramped and dingy, strewn with dog-eared magazines and grimy, broken toys; rooms that simply did not measure up. When she first came to work in this practice, eleven years ago, she liked this room immediately. She still appreciates its good proportions; the northern light through the large windows that gives a feel of austere comfort, a restrained yet calming aesthetic, exactly what a doctor's waiting room should project. It makes a good impression, this room. She has always believed in the value of making a good impression.

Behind the reception desk Margaret is on the phone, dealing with the Monday rush. They make eye contact, exchange knowing nods. She picks up the first patient's file from her tray. The name is not familiar but when she calls it — *Lisa Salvatore* — she vaguely recognises the young woman who puts aside a magazine and rises from her seat to follow her down the corridor to her consulting room. At the door to her room she waits, gesturing with her hand and a small inclination of her head, for her patient to enter. Such well-worn habits: her upturned hand, her small tight smile as she makes eye contact with the young woman — her name is Lisa, she must remember it when addressing her — who smiles briefly in return. The stiff familiarity of the vaguely recognised patient, neither old patient nor new. Old patients, loyal to the grave, are prepared to forgive their doctor anything. New patients have no preconceptions. Lisa settles herself in the chair, her handbag on her lap. She looks in the file for the date of Lisa's last consultation. It was eighteen months ago. Has Lisa been well over the past eighteen months, or, more likely, has she been doing the rounds?

Lisa has come for a repeat pill prescription. The same one she was taking when last seen at this clinic? No, it was changed by another doctor at another clinic, some eleven months ago. Ah! It is just as she suspected. And will that be all? No: Lisa feels as if her neck might be swollen. Her mother has commented on it. Lisa puts her hands to her thyroid gland. From across the desk, the young woman's thyroid looks a little enlarged, but, then, she does not know how it looked before. In answer to her questions, Lisa tells her there is no pain or difficulty swallowing. There are no constitutional symptoms, apart from occasional tiredness, which can almost always be discounted. Everyone is tired these days. And yet tiredness can be a symptom of significant disease: leukaemia, diabetes, renal failure, depression. Nothing can ever be fully discounted. She stands behind Lisa, who still clutches her handbag—if body language is any guide, this reticence to discard her bag is not a good sign—and palpates the thyroid from behind, as she was taught to do as a student. Those distant days of medical school, when examining patients was a novelty and nothing more, a harmless routine to be rehearsed in one's own time, at one's own pace—though now she pities those frail old women, captive in unforgiving hospital beds, on whose arthritic hips or failing hearts she clumsily practised her craft. These days a physical examination carries with it the weight of diagnosis, of getting it right. She is no longer sure she can get it right, at least not every time.

'We will do a blood test to check your thyroid function and an ultrasound of your neck to get a clearer picture of what is going on,' she says to Lisa. She is conscious of using 'we' instead of 'I'. Is she hiding behind fictitious others, trying to protect herself from being singled out for criticism? If so, it will not work. 'And a couple of other blood tests to check your tiredness.' Hang the expense, she thinks. Isn't this what patients want: a thorough going-over? No room for uncertainty. No stone left unturned. She stands and sees Lisa to the door, then returns to her desk to write a few notes.

Before this all happened, before the writ was served, before the lawyers had her phone numbers—at a time when it now seems that all decisions fell lightly and easily into place—every consultation was simply an analysis of the patient's problem. She would think in terms of the patient's agenda, of what it was the patient wanted from the fifteen-minute interaction. Whether she would be able to provide the patient with what they wanted was another matter, but at least they would both know where they stood. During the consultation she would construct hypotheses, not only about the diagnosis of the presenting problem but also the patient's real reasons for coming, the patient's hidden concerns. She would use her communication skills, her medical knowledge, a certain level of intuition to tap into the patient's health belief system; she would read body language, interpret the Freudian slip of the tongue, the use of key words. She projected outwards, towards her patient; in counselling parlance, she empathised. In her own modest way she could read minds. Now, as her patients talk, she turns inward, analysing her risk of exposure. She has spent so long with lawyers she is beginning to think in their terms.

February 20

Her last patient of the day is a forty-nine-year-old woman called Susan, new to the clinic. Susan explains how she is struggling with symptoms of the menopause. 'I am so tired,' Susan tells her. 'Tired through to my bones. And still I can't sleep. I barely get four hours a night.' Susan's voice trails away and she begins to cry.

She places the tissue box within Susan's reach and waits while she wipes her eyes. She sees the consultation path stretching out before her: the exploration of Susan's tiredness will lead to questions about lifestyle, work and family. Her husband's attitudes and behaviours will be ever so gently probed. She will ask about Pap smears and breast checks, and encourage Susan in healthy habits. *Take time out for yourself*, she will say. They will circle the topic of hormone therapy: she will be cautious not to advocate it, even though she suspects this is why Susan has come. Even so, she will not prescribe it today, not without first sending Susan away, replete with handouts, to decide for herself. Hormone replacement has lately become a minefield of risks, a quagmire of qualifications. Doctors must tread carefully, and no one more carefully than she.

She can do all this, the peri-menopausal consultation, with her eyes closed. At this moment that is exactly what she would like to do: close her eyes and her ears, too, and rest her head upon the desk. She, also, is tired to her bones but, unlike Susan, she cannot find the time or see the need to burden someone else with her woes.

Before she leaves work she runs through the appointment diary on the computer, as is now her daily habit. She adds up the patients who, at review, have responded to her treatment, plus those who felt better by the time they left her room. The sum is disappointingly small. With a sinking heart she also tallies the patients whose cough has got worse, whose rash has spread, despite her interventions. *Would they have been better off if I had done nothing?* she asks herself each evening as she walks to her car. *Would they have been better off seeing someone else?*

Before Ben Feltham she had believed, had she ever stopped to consider it, that on the whole the medical profession did good: lives saved, diseases prevented and cured, suffering ameliorated. How could she have continued in her profession if she had believed otherwise? Of course there were times, isolated events, when the harm done by a doctor outweighed the good. In her days as a resident there were the occasional catastrophes, procedural mishaps: the misplacement of a central venous line, for example; the cannula failing to enter the internal jugular vein, instead puncturing the apex of the lung and causing it to collapse with a soft *hiss* like a leaking balloon. And, infrequently, misdiagnoses that led to permanent disability, or even death.

She often thinks now of one particular woman, a patient in her care during the first few months of her intern year. She does not remember her name, that unassuming woman who came alone to the hospital one evening with bad left-sided subcostal pain. She had not been present when the woman arrived but she later heard the story from the intern who had first seen the woman in emergency. The woman told the intern she had been the driver in a car accident, several days before. Just a minor one, the woman said: no injuries sustained, save for a little bruising. This was duly recorded in the emergency-room notes; recorded then forgotten. After the physical examination the intern ordered, amongst other tests, a chest X-ray. The films came back with some changes in the lower lobe of the left lung, the same site as the woman's pain. Could she have pneumonia? No one in emergency was quite sure and, being after-hours, the radiologist was not there to report on the films. The woman had no cough or fever: what then to make of it?

The medical registrar was called down from the wards for his opinion. 'Does it hurt when you breathe in?' he had asked the woman. The doctors in emergency had not asked this question; had not thought to ask it. 'Yes,' she replied. He took her pulse and noted it was fast. *Pleuritic chest pain, tachycardia*, the registrar wrote in the emergency notes. *Diagnosis: pulmonary embolism* was written below. A blood clot in the lung. The patient would go to the medical ward for anti-coagulation.

At that moment, when the registrar announced his diagnosis to the emergency-room staff and the admitting officer picked up the phone to find a bed on the medical ward, the woman's pain, until then undifferentiated, now had a label. Her constellation of signs and symptoms, and the finding on her chest X-ray—that hazy lung opacity that, in retrospect, could have meant many different things—were gathered together under one diagnosis and labelled as 'medical'. The woman was deemed to have a medical problem, rather than a surgical one. These days, as a generalist, as one who claims to treat the whole patient, she sees this rigid separation of the medical from the surgical as a dangerous practice, though one common in resident doctors, at least of her time. Is it any different now? Do hospital doctors take a more holistic approach, or do they, as she once did, still label and separate—the liver from the lungs, the head from the heart, the body from the mind? She knows nothing of teaching hospitals now, except what her patients tell her: dirty bathrooms, harried nurses. In her day the bathrooms were clean and nurses thick on the ground. Have the hospital doctors changed, too? She suspects very little, if at all.

In the medical ward, two days later, the woman was still in pain. Her lung scan had been equivocal but still the heparin ran, drop by drop, into her bloodstream. She still remembers, or at least thinks she remembers, the expression on the woman's face during the ward round that morning. An expression of fear: fear of suffering, perhaps, or else an intuitive fear that the diagnosis of pulmonary embolism was incorrect. When later that day the woman's condition deteriorated—her blood pressure and haemoglobin fell, indicating internal bleeding—and a surgical opinion was urgently sought, it was decided the woman was suffering, not with a pulmonary embolism, but from a surgical problem: that of a ruptured spleen, no doubt sustained in the car accident, during impact, as the seat belt pressed into her abdomen. She was rushed to theatre for an emergency laparotomy and there, as the surgeon had predicted, was found to have a ruptured spleen; the bleeding, increased by the anti-coagulation therapy, still contained within the fibrous confines of the splenic capsule. Her spleen was removed, she was transfused and, by the skin of her teeth, she survived.

The balance between harm and good: in this woman's case, so precariously poised. Had she not been correctly diagnosed at that particular hour, had her blood—thinned and depleted by the heparin prescribed by her doctors, herself included: the order in her own handwriting on the chart at the foot of the woman's bed—been left an hour, even thirty minutes longer to strain the walls of the splenic capsule to bursting point, it is possible she would have died of haemorrhage, massive and uncontrollable. One might argue that, despite regrettable delay, this woman *was* correctly diagnosed and managed. That her ruptured spleen was initially difficult to diagnose; that, on the balance of the presenting history and examination, she was diagnosed with a *probable* condition, the treatment of which *unfortunately* exacerbated the *actual* condition from which she suffered. (Listen to her! She is thinking like a lawyer, doggedly pursuing each strand of the argument. Well, what does it matter? If she can think like them, so much the better.) That, despite the initial misdiagnosis, the medical and nursing staff were not the *cause* of her ruptured spleen. That, despite what happened during the first two days of her hospital admission—her pain, her fear, her unheeded bleeding—she left hospital having been managed appropriately: her surgical wound healing well, her haemoglobin normalised. But one would be foolish, or simply callous, to take this line of argument; to focus only on outcome, ignoring the flaws in the process, trivialising the suffering of the patient who, for two days, lay quietly in her hospital bed, afraid of her pain but even more fearful of its underlying cause, of the possible harm being done: harm both instigated by her own damaged body and inflicted upon her by doctors, by those who inserted the intravenous cannula, by those whose signature had consigned her to possible death by exsanguination.

Were there legal ramifications? Not in that case. Although she had examined the patient herself and written up the orders for heparin, she was never held to account or asked to explain. Of course there were other ramifications: the open scorn of the surgical team, the stigma of incompetence that dogged the medical registrar for the remainder of the year. She told the story to the other interns, making herself out, as only a first year could, to be an innocent bystander in the affair. *She* did not make the diagnosis. *She* was only following orders. Wasn't *she* the one who had alerted the registrar to the poor woman's falling haemoglobin? At the time she believed she had learned something valuable from the whole unfortunate episode, though exactly what that was she would have been hard pressed to explain. But perhaps she did not learn anything much at all. Perhaps if she *had* learned something, instead of thinking about saving her own skin, she would not now have a lawsuit hanging over her head.

She is not, has never been, nostalgic for her residency days. At twenty-seven she was happy to leave the strange, closeted other-world of the hospital for a life in general practice, where there was sunlight through the windows and noises from the street, where patients could come and go as they chose. But she can now see there is some advantage to be had in the hospital as an institution: an advantage for doctors, that is. During her residency, when patients were harmed, the erring doctors' trials were conducted within the confines of the hospital, away from the public eye. Lawyers had nothing to do with it. The doctors' mistakes, however grave, were at least seen in some sort of context. Lack of experience, fatigue secondary to overwork, exacerbated by lack of supervision, the need to make quick decisions, to take urgent action: contributory factors that all other doctors experientially understood. To be judged by one's peers, however harshly, was to be judged within the context of one's situation: that of a young adult, just twenty-five years old, battling physical and mental fatigue, sometimes overwhelmed, even frightened, by the nature of the work, pressured over the phone by a sleep-deprived registrar, with no training in mentoring, to do something—make a decision, undertake a procedure—of which one was unsure, ill-equipped. (Those interminable nights on the wards as an intern: her lonely footsteps on the linoleum floors, a torch in her hand. She would pull back the bedside curtains and shine the torch into the patient's face. *A rabbit caught in the headlights.* What tortures she inflicted!) Such were the circumstances of the resident doctor and, under such circumstances, mistakes were made. Could anyone else have done better?

In the residents' lounge, around a table strewn with the leftovers of cafeteria dinners, she and her fellow juniors, her compatriots, would discuss the failings of the system of which they were a part—on the lowest rung of the ladder, grist to the mill. They would lampoon consultants, delight in shameful stories about the most hated of registrars, all the while ready to push back their chairs and break into a run—down the walkway and into the wards—whenever a 'code red' was called. The voice over the PA would be mellifluous, soothing: what hospital visitor, sitting at their relative's bedside, would have guessed that in a nearby ward, the curtains drawn around them, someone lay unconscious, close to death? 'Code Red 4 South, Code Red 4 South.' How they would run, their shoes clattering down the walkway, striding up the stairs two at a time, clutching their stethoscopes; they were so young, so raw! But when it came down to it, they—she—had lacked the courage to challenge the system. Was courage all it took? If she had overthrown the system, what would she have replaced it with? What would she replace it with now? She is in no position to judge.

Yet there was a camaraderie, wasn't there? The dressing-down from their seniors, the scorn of the charge nurses, blood and excrement and grimness their daily routine: they were all in it together. Through shared experience one's peers understood how mistakes might be made. They recognised in others—because they saw it in themselves—those finely tissued layers of human behaviour: duty, pride, overconfidence, fatigue-driven indecision, fear of failure, fear of doing harm. One's peers understood and, in their own begrudging way, forgave. It is a different thing, she suspects, to be judged by a court, by a judge who knows only the weight of evidence, the rigour of argument; a judge who knows nothing of the visceral, who does not know what it is to see a patient die, who has never heard, with one's shaking hand holding the cannula, the *sigh* of a collapsing lung, who does not understand the intrinsic truth of being a doctor: that, while the mind may deceive, the body does not.

A negligence suit. The phrase still makes her shudder. She thinks of the brown suit worn by the young man who served her the writ. Three years ago next month: William had been seven, Joe just four. It was in the waiting room, in front of her patients, on what had been, up until that moment, an ordinary morning. As she had entered to call her next patient, the young man had stood and walked towards her, a sheaf of papers under his arm. She saw how his suit jacket strained tight across his bulging stomach and how his trousers, slung low under his paunch, sat in soft folds against his shoes. He walked with the swagger of a minor official, someone who had let a little authority go straight to his head. A drug rep, she had thought, less well-groomed than most. An overweight drug rep in a cheap, ill-fitting suit. She was about to tell him she could not see him without an appointment, but he spoke first; a sentence or two in a nasal monotone. She remembers only his sour breath on her face, not what he said. And yet already she understood his errand. Ben Feltham had come to find her. She realised, then, that she had been expecting him.

A negligence suit. She wears one now: a cheap suit that chafes and itches, one that is not easily removed, even after hours. A suit of sackcloth and ashes. Would that her penance be only this, but she knows there is more to come.

February 21

After work she picks the boys up from school and takes them, complaining, to their appointment with the new dentist. William's teeth are fine, but Joe needs a filling. Defective enamel, the dentist tells her. Joe also has a tongue-tie. Didn't she already know that? He asks Joe to poke out his tongue. 'See how his tongue is tethered here?' He indicates the problem, touching the underside of Joe's tongue with one of his delicate metal probes.

She sees, now, that the tip of the tongue curves back under itself, the frenulum tightly reining it in. 'I must confess that I've never noticed it before,' she says.

'It will need to be released, if only for cosmetic reasons,' the dentist tells her. 'In the old days you'd simply snip it in your rooms, wouldn't you?'

'Not in my day, or my rooms,' she replies. The dentist shouldn't speak so flippantly in front of a child. She squeezes Joe's hand. 'Don't worry,' she tells him. 'It's just a little thing and easily fixed. We'll talk about it when we get home.'

It is now her turn in the chair. She has barely stretched open her mouth before she senses the dentist is not pleased with her. His forehead is creased into a frown, his eyes narrowed as he probes around her teeth. The rest of his face is hidden by his mask. At times the probe seems to go very deeply into her jaw. Blood begins to trickle down her throat. The dentist draws back sharply for a few seconds and glances at his dental nurse. Maybe the smell of her breath has overwhelmed him.

After a few minutes the dentist puts aside his instruments and lowers his mask. 'Your gums are in a terrible condition. Have you noticed how swollen and inflamed they are? A good deal of the periodontal bone and ligaments have been eaten away by inflammation. You're in serious danger of losing a few teeth. Some of your fillings will also need to be replaced, but that can wait.'

From the corner of her eye she is aware of the boys' fidgeting. She lifts her head from the chair to see William grab at Joe's arm as he reaches for a large plastic tooth sitting on the bench, a model of an impeccably white molar set in candy-pink gum. For their sakes she has always tried to downplay a visit to the dentist. Her children shouldn't have to hear such emotive language, such negative language in the dental surgery.

'Go and wait outside,' she tells them, straining her neck to catch Joe's eye. She hopes she does not have blood around her mouth. 'I will be out soon.'

'What do I have to do?' she asks, when the boys have gone.

'You'll need to see a periodontist, and quickly. Your condition is too advanced for me to fix. It must have been going on for quite a while. Didn't your last dentist ever mention any of this to you?'

At home she examines her mouth in the bathroom mirror. She can see, now, that the gums are an unhealthy crimson, swollen and boggy, and that the gum edge has retracted from its original position around the teeth. The back teeth are most affected: the gum around the molars has shrunk away until the roots of the teeth, chalky and yellow, have become exposed. It seems surprising, more than surprising, that she has not noticed this before. There has been bleeding when she brushes, bright blood, mixed with toothpaste, in the basin: she has seen *that*. But how is it that, cleaning her teeth in front of the mirror each morning, she has continually failed to see what she now sees so clearly: the fiery, swollen gums, the disfigured teeth?

That evening, while peeling potatoes for a curry, it occurs to her that the new dentist does not know how to give bad news. Doctors have often been accused of the same thing. Although such a task is never pleasant, always imperfectly executed, she has tried to do it as best she can: giving the patient time to ask questions, trying to ensure their spouse is at their side, emphasising the advancements in treatment. *Medical research is moving along in leaps and bounds*, she will say, and she imagines white-coated boffins vaulting laboratory benches. She is careful not to extinguish hope. In the most hopeless cases—the diagnosis of motor neurone disease, carcinomas of the liver or pancreas—hope must remain. In the most hopeless cases, what else is there to offer but hope?

She did not offer Ben Feltham hope. She should add that mistake to the others. The phone call about him, the first of many, had come while she was with a patient.

'It looks like an osteosarcoma of the distal femur,' the radiologist said. 'Can I send them back to see you now?'

'Of course. I will see them straight away.' She put down the phone and continued the consultation. When the patient left the room she quickly searched the internet. Osteosarcoma was rare, she read on an American cancer site, so rare that the diagnosis was often initially missed. There were patients' stories of delayed diagnoses but she chose not to read them. Margaret soon rang to tell her the Felthams had arrived. 'I'm coming,' she said but she stayed in her room, again scanning the internet, hoping the same word—*osteosarcoma*—would this time yield something new, something promising. What had she been looking for? Perhaps, already, some line of defence.

She went out to the waiting room where they were sitting: Ben, staring at the floor, his head in his hands, and his mother, holding the X-rays. Ben's mother looked up as she approached. She met his mother's eyes, trying to look professional; concerned yet in control. Wasn't that the best image to project? She was thinking on her feet. She had already decided that she should be careful. Once inside her room she told them the provisional diagnosis. 'There will need to be confirmatory scans and a biopsy, but the X-ray is fairly conclusive.' She held the film to the viewing box, and showed them the tumour: the punched-out oval, marked with the radiologist's pencil, in the lower femoral shaft, almost as if a bubble of air was trapped in the bone. No longer able to look at it, she switched off the viewing box and handed the X-ray back to his mother. She had missed it. She had missed his cancer.

'How long has it been there?' his mother asked.

She said she did not know. She was already retreating. She was in unfamiliar territory, behind enemy lines.

'What happens now?'

She dared not talk about treatment, except in the most general terms. Never had she been so ill-prepared. 'I will speak to an orthopaedic surgeon. They will see Ben as soon as possible. I will let you know this afternoon.' She had no printed material to give them, no website address she could confidently recommend. Osteosarcoma was so rare. Was it listed in her general-practice textbook, sitting on the shelf behind her, as one of those rare diseases that should not be missed? That one could not afford to miss? Common things are common but rare things still occur. She had not thought to ask him about night-time pain: the hallmark of bony malignancy. She wanted them to leave. She needed more time to prepare herself. She sensed the fear taking hold of them—the boy's fear more nebulous and slow, his mother's sharp and dangerous—yet did nothing to help. She had given bad news before and had done it well, coaxing fear out into the open where it could be cornered and stared down. But never before had she missed a diagnosis like this. *The boy had had symptoms for seven months.* How could she lay claim to being helpful when she had already made the situation far worse? She should have said sorry then, said the word a thousand times over, but she had been too afraid to speak.

February 25

Her solicitor, John Trumble, phones her at work to let her know the date for mediation has been set for the twenty-eighth of May. 'We will need to meet beforehand, closer to the date, to go over things once more.'

'Again?' She hears the strain in her voice. 'Surely there's no more to discuss. I've told you everything I know.'

There is a pause on the other end of the line; time enough for her to reflect on what she has just said. Is she behaving badly? Is she being uncooperative? Do they, these medical defence lawyers, have in-house terms for their doctor clients: 'unreliable witness', 'uncooperative defendant'? How has she been labelled? 'Difficult'— a 'difficult woman'?

'Mediation is a very important part of the process,' John eventually replies. 'One-fifth of cases are settled at this point.' He pauses briefly. Is he choosing his words? 'And, in the event that settlement is *not* reached, the meeting with the plaintiff still gives us the opportunity to review their case *in vivo*, so to speak. It's therefore in your best interests that we endeavour to cross all the t's and dot all the i's prior to the event.'

'Of course. I understand.' She tries to sound penitent. Despite the fact that he peppers his speech with an endless collection of legalistic clichés—desiccated phrases that ring ominously hollow—he is only trying to help: she must keep remembering that. 'When would you like to meet?'

She dreads these meetings. Of course she would like to forget all about the case, if such a thing were possible. She cannot forget but neither does she want to be reminded, in such excruciating detail, at every encounter. She writes down the date of the meeting, feeling deep within her such a resistance to the process that she is concerned she might actually have recorded the date incorrectly. Is such dread, such resistance, what anyone would feel in her place, or is she particularly affected? It is difficult to know: there is no one with whom to compare notes. No one she knows personally has ever been sued; at least, she thinks not. Who are they, where are they, these other doctors in her position? Keeping their heads down, trying to get on with it, just as she is doing.

'You're a vital member of the team,' John had told her at their first encounter. 'Your inside knowledge of the case is of great use to the rest of us.' She assumed he had been trying to put her at ease—but his choice of words! He spoke as if it had been her intention to gain such inside knowledge, as if knowledge of the case were all that mattered. *I would rather be in your shoes than mine*, she had wanted to say. Besides, she has never been a team player: never wanted to be, if the truth be told. Even at school, on sports afternoons, she always preferred tennis to netball or hockey. The jostling and shouting of a netball game, the outstretched arms, the back-slapping, made her feel uncomfortably detached, somehow fraudulent, but in a game of tennis, especially a singles match, she always knew exactly where she stood.

Most doctors are the same, she suspects: individualists, unwilling or unable to work by consensus. Doesn't her solicitor realise this by now? He must have had enough experience of them to see how they steer their own course, beholden to no one but their patients. And sometimes, not even their patients. But more to the point, it seems John cannot see the differences in the way he and she approach the conference table. He is a lawyer who has chosen to specialise in medical defence; she and her situation are simply part of his job. He need not lose a wink of sleep over her predicament. He does not know, for she has not told him, that the night before these meetings she barely sleeps. Neither has she told him that sometimes—as he questions her again on the details of the case and she stumbles over her replies, staring with smarting eyes at the pages of medical notes in an attempt to find some new interpretation of the words written there, in her own handwriting; a fresh interpretation that will miraculously clear her of all fault—she feels as if she were being physically assailed with blows, or as if she were a piece of road kill, a rotting carcass being picked dry by crows. Of course she will not tell him: he is on her side, after all. But if she feels like this now, how will she cope when the prosecution starts in upon her?

When she gets home Paul is sitting at the computer while the boys watch television in the next room. In the kitchen the breakfast dishes are still in the sink and there is no sign that dinner has been started. At Paul's bidding she returns to the study and stands behind him, looking at the computer screen. He is setting up a file for her taxation records, he tells her. She needs to see the accountant soon: the closing date for last year's tax return is fast approaching. It is true that, over recent months, she has neglected her finances, just as she has neglected other things—dinners with friends, reading for pleasure. How she hates that word, *neglect*. Must everything she does, or does not do, now be tinged with fault? And yet it is the word that comes to her, over and over. Paul talks as he moves and clicks the mouse, demonstrating the various functions of the accounting program. She tries to concentrate, but her eyes eventually stray from the screen to the top of his head. She sees, for the first time, that his hair is thinning at the crown. Is he aware of this? Probably not, as it is only visible from above. Should she tell him? Entirely out of context, the words *duty of disclosure* come to mind. If she tells him now, in the middle of his demonstration, he will be annoyed. It will seem to him that she is not paying attention, not valuing his time and knowledge. Not only that: he might think she is trying to belittle him by criticising his physical appearance. But to tell him later, to hoard the information, would be to attribute some importance to her discovery. And, of course, it is not important. Nevertheless, he might still like to know, might like to consider treatment at this early stage. It would be easier to pretend she has not seen it, this small circle of scalp visible through the thinning strands of hair. She stares at the top of his head, not knowing how to act, what to say.

Over dinner — a vegetarian pasta, so hastily prepared that the onions are not properly cooked — Paul tells her he has been nominated for an Institute award, in the sustainable-architecture category. She congratulates him and leans across the table to kiss him on the cheek. She tries to look and sound as pleased as she can.

The nomination is for a low-rise office building in the Docklands area, at the city's edge. She knows he is proud of this building: prouder of this than any other project of his career. She has seen the building only once, soon after it was completed, on a wet Sunday afternoon last year in winter. After a visit to the city museum they had caught a tram to Docklands. The rain ran down the rattling windows and the tram shuddered in the southerly crosswind as it left the city and descended to the docks area, open and windswept, the grey skies expansive. Paul's building was a beacon in the rain; low-slung and cantilevered, humorous. The boys had laughed at its curved orange walls, although she had thought it made perfect sense to have something bright and shapely in this grey, flat place. 'Who chose the colour?' she had asked. She hoped it had been him, as it would have confirmed him as an optimist and iconoclast. She wanted to believe he was still both of these things.

Paul tells her the award will be announced at the annual Institute dinner. She has been to these dinners before, but never as the wife of a nominee.

'When is it?' she asks.

'The twenty-eighth of May.'

Her first instinct is to tell him she cannot go. That the twenty-eighth is the day of her mediation hearing: she cannot possibly be expected to go out that evening. But she bites her tongue. This is Paul's moment, not hers. If his career is going well, so much the better. At least one of them is good at their job.

February 26

She phones the new dental surgery and asks to speak to the dentist.

'You said my condition had been present for some time. Do you mean months, or years?'

'Years. Maybe as long as ten years. You've got chronic inflammation there.'

'I last saw my previous dentist eighteen months ago. Could the problem have developed since then?'

The dentist does not hesitate. 'No. You would have had evidence of disease long before that.'

Her previous dentist, Brian Leonard, retired last July. For almost forty years she made her annual visit to the large Edwardian house that was his surgery, first with her mother and later by herself. And when William and Joe were each three years old, she had taken them with her. On those first visits with the boys her own childhood memories had flooded back, so that the pebbles on the path that wound through the garden crunched and scraped more loudly underfoot and, as they opened the front door, the automatic buzzer seemed to sound with a new ferocity. And that smell of antiseptic! The boys noticed it, too. Were the floors cleaned with it? She remembers the quiet gloom of the waiting room, illuminated to a half-light, even on the sunniest days, by an old glass chandelier that hung from the yellowing ceiling. The bookcase held some comics and a book of illustrated Bible stories that endured for many years. There were quaint ornaments on a shelf: a frilly crystal bowl holding blown-glass fruit, and a family of china dogs, collecting dust. In a corner of the room was a large fish tank, and there on its sandy bed, almost hidden by waving water plants, stood a deep-sea diver figurine in an old-fashioned diving suit. Now and then a soft flurry of air bubbles rose from the diver's helmet and the tank made a gentle humming sound as the goldfish swam, back and forth, unperturbed by the diver's breathing. Her mother had once told her the fish tank was there to soothe the nerves of the patients—adults and children alike—as they sat in that dimly lit room, listening to the ticking of the old carriage clock on the mantle, awaiting their turn to be called by the nurse, to follow her squeaking shoes down the corridor and into the dentist's surgery. The surgery itself was a shining sanctum. Sunlight poured in through a skylight in the ceiling and the stainless steel benches glinted, reflecting patches of light onto the walls. In the centre of the room was the dentist's chair. There presided Doctor Leonard in his buttoned white tunic.

But *she* had not been afraid of the dentist. Her mother had been careful never to speak of him in any way that might provoke anxiety, and dental appointments were kept secret until the day before. Perhaps, too, the fish tank worked its hypnotic, associative spell so effectively that the thought of a dental appointment immediately conjured feelings of tranquillity. As a child she'd had her share of caries, and she knew each time she sat in the chair that the chance of a filling, and all it entailed, was reasonably high. (Perhaps, like Joe, she too had defective enamel.) But, despite this less than easy course, despite the occasional twinge of pain as the drill escaped the boundaries of the local anaesthetic, she does not remember being afraid. Surely her courage counted for something?

March 2

She has arranged to meet her mother for lunch at a café in the public gardens. As she approaches the café she spots her mother sitting at an outside table, reading a book. She points her out to William and Joe, who run ahead to greet their grandmother. While the boys hold her mother's hands and talk excitedly over each other, she slips quietly into a seat at the table.

Her mother turns from the children to greet her. She is wearing a straw sunhat with a pink bow, and matching lipstick. 'What a lovely day,' she says brightly.

She knows this is not what her mother wants to say, that the lipstick and sunhat are foils of a sort: that her mother is trying, for her sake, to tread carefully, to keep the mood light. But she does not feel comforted. She cannot even summon the slightest sense of gratitude, heartless daughter that she is.

'How is Paul?' her mother asks, after they have ordered lunch and the boys have run off to practise handstands on the grass.

'He's playing golf today. He says hello.'

'Golf? I didn't know he played.'

'He's only recently taken it up.' As to why he has done this, has taken to leaving the house early Sunday morning to return mid-afternoon, sunburned and evasive, she does not speculate, at least not with her mother. She, too, must tread carefully.

They talk about her younger sister, Sophie, who is soon to have her first baby.

'Have you seen her recently?' her mother asks.

It is a perfectly reasonable question, yet she feels herself bristling. 'About two weeks ago.' Whether or not this qualifies as recent she is not prepared to guess.

'She's having some trouble with her back, but I'm sure she's told you all about it.'

No, she does not believe that Sophie has mentioned it. Then again, it is possible she has forgotten, just as now, with some of her patients—especially those who tend to complain—she forgets their symptoms only minutes after they have recounted them. She has never minded that her family consult her informally on medical matters: in fact, she would rather they asked her advice than not. But, in some way or another, Sophie's back pain has passed her by. Well, maybe it is for the best.

Just as they are about to leave the table, her mother reaches for her bag and unzips a side pocket, from which she produces a small colour photo.

'I found this the other day. Don't you think it's so like William? It's the expression, I think, more than anything else.'

She takes the photo from her mother. It is a picture of her as a child at what appears to be a picnic. Spread in front of her, on a brown checked rug, is an assortment of food: a plate of sandwiches, cut into tiny triangles; a plate of iced patty cakes; a packet of chocolate biscuits. She is looking at the camera with a serious, slightly haughty expression, as if she has been interrupted in the middle of an absorbing or difficult task. 'I'm not sure I can see William in it,' she says. William, her eldest, as she was the eldest. The seriousness of the eldest child: is this what her mother is implying? She hands the photo back across the table.

'No,' says her mother. 'I want you to keep it.'

At home she looks at the photograph again. Try as she might, she cannot retrieve any memories of the day on which it was taken. Did her mother take the photo? What prompted her at that moment, in the midst of that picnic, to put aside her coffee cup and pull the old camera from its brown leather case? What did her mother see, or think she saw, through the viewing window? At the age of sixty-eight, her mother is still in good health but one day — who knows, perhaps soon — her health will fail. At first a minor complaint, barely worth a mention, then the gradual stuttering decline into frailty, senility. She must ask her mother to write her autobiography while her hand is still firm and while she still remembers. But it is not her mother's story that she longs to hear. Rather, it is the story of the eldest daughter, told as a fairy tale, all goodness and kindness, and with a happy ending.

March 3

A mother brings in her two-year-old son for an overdue vaccination. As the needle enters the boy's flesh, he lets out a scream of rage and jerks his arm out of his mother's grasp. The needle dislodges and somehow, in the ruckus, ends up pricking the tip of her finger. Her first thought is that the boy's mother must not know. She gets the mother to hold a cotton-wool swab to the sobbing boy's arm while she goes to the basin. Half the dose of vaccine remains in the syringe. Should she give the boy a second injection, with all the drama that would entail? What would his mother think? She discards the syringe in the sharps container and washes her hands. With her back to the woman, she quickly applies a plaster over the needle-stick site, on which a drop of blood has beaded. She is not particularly concerned about the injury: what blood-borne virus could a healthy two-year-old give her? But the whole episode has shaken her. After the boy has gone, she again washes her finger and dabs it with antiseptic, then sits at her desk with a thumping heart. Poor injection technique and a needle-stick injury: incompetence, in anyone's book.

She has not had a needle-stick injury since her resident days. Now she thinks back to one in particular, during her second year of residency, her three-month stint on the gastrointestinal ward. She cannot recall whether she was taking blood when it happened, or whether it was during a certain investigative procedure, when the lights were often dimmed for X-ray contrast and, in the gloom, it was difficult to see the tip of a needle. What she does remember is that the woman, with whose blood she was inoculated, had an unexplained condition: an inflammation of the liver that could not be diagnosed with the investigations then available. She also recalls how the tip of the needle jammed deeply into the pulp of her thumb, hitting bone, so that for days afterwards her thumb was tender to the touch. She did not report the injury, knowing there was nothing to be gained, that her registrar would think she was clumsy and incompetent, that she had brought the injury upon herself. The patient did not have hepatitis B or HIV, she reasoned, so there was no obvious cause for alarm. Yet for weeks afterwards she would press the tip of her thumb, squeezing hard into the fleshy pulp, wondering what nature of biological matter had been deposited there, when the needle pierced her skin and entered deep into soft tissue.

What exactly had she been thinking? Was it fear that made her passive? Or was it, instead, a kind of recklessness? She had been prepared to watch and wait, to take her chances. To play a kind of Russian roulette: micro-organisms in place of bullets, a needle in place of a pistol. She has since had further blood tests, including a test for hepatitis C, and now knows, in as much as anyone can know given the information currently available, that she is in the clear. So her gamble paid off, in that case at least. But there have been other times she has gambled, she realises now, sitting at her desk, her head in her hands while time marches on. Gambled to lose, rather than to win.

That young woman, Claire. Must she go over this now? Three years ago. Three years, give or take a month or two. A month can be a long time in a woman's life. Claire had come to see her with a fever and a rash: a common presentation, bread-and-butter medicine. Except that Claire was also pregnant: thirty-seven weeks, close to term. As Claire lifted her shirt to display the fine pink spots that stippled her abdomen she had witnessed, as clear as day, the imprint of a tiny fist pushing upwards against its fleshy confines. A gesture of rebellion, perhaps. She told Claire she had a viral infection. *Non-specific*, she had said. A no-name virus: any fool could have diagnosed that. Her baby would be unaffected: all, in short, would be well. As if to prove it, she had held the foetal doppler to Claire's belly and, as her baby's heart beat its tom-tom around the room, Claire had smiled. The heartbeat was fast but, then, Claire had a fever.

It was only later that day she let herself think of other more sinister possibilities, other infections — quite *specific* infections, in fact — that could cross the placenta to infect the foetus. Toxoplasmosis, rubella, cytomegalovirus, herpes simplex. To admit these possibilities was to admit to their sequelae: deafness, encephalitis, mental retardation. Claire's baby might not be so safe, after all.

That evening, before leaving work, she picked up the phone to summon Claire back—there were things to be said and done, tests to be ordered, prescriptions to write—but put it down again before dialling the number. At the time she sensed a resistance deep within, a hard core of something akin to indifference that forced the receiver from her hand and back into its cradle. She told herself she was simply tired and in a fractious frame of mind, perhaps even a little anaemic. After all, she had lost some blood the week before. She would even go so far as to say—in her clinical opinion—a considerable amount of blood. For Claire's sake, she would not overreact. It would be wrong to frighten her. All would be well.

The next day she again thought about talking to Claire and yet she did not, nor the day after that. The tussle continued day after day until it was too late: too late to turn back, too late to make an admission of ... what, exactly? One night she dreamed she saw a baby drowning—in a giant bath or a swimming pool. The water was smooth and milky, almost opaque. As its body submerged it raised a tiny fist in a gesture of supplication. Or it might have been rebellion.

Ten weeks later she saw Claire again, for a postnatal check. When she examined Claire's six-week-old daughter, she held an infant who was neither deaf nor blind; who, at the sound of her mother's voice, had turned her head and smiled.

Why? Why did she do nothing? Was it some kind

of insane gamble: her knowledge wagered against the natural course of the infection, whatever it might have turned out to be? She has never been a risk-taker and yet this behaviour—cavalier, dangerous, negligent. If only those lawyers knew. In this wager of such high stakes, if that is what it was, what did she stand to gain? The stakes surely reflect the value of the prize. What, then, was worth such risks? She still struggles with this, knowing the answer is concerned with something fundamental, something with roots that have grown long and deep and intertwined: that to bring the answer to the surface, to *uproot* it, means exposing aspects of herself she does not wish to expose. *A psychotherapist would make mincemeat of me*, she thinks. *If I had to confess, what would I say?*

This is getting her nowhere. She has patients to see. Despite her inaction, all was well in the end. She had been tired, maybe a little anaemic. Let her leave it at that and get on with the day.

There is a pile of paperwork in her in-tray that she must attend to, so she lets the evening receptionist go home and stays on alone at her desk. Save for the rustling of her papers and the scratching of her pen, the clinic is strangely quiet: no telephones, no babies' cries, no voices in the corridor. She looks up from a letter at the wail of a siren; in the distance, at first, then moving closer and closer, louder and louder, until it sounds as if it is right outside the clinic door. She bolts from her room and down the corridor, just in time to see the flashing lights

of an ambulance through the waiting-room window.
Her heart is pounding. The ambulance continues on its
way. She waits as the sound of the siren recedes, then
goes to the kitchen for some water. Her hand shakes as
she raises the glass to her lips. What was she afraid of?
Did she really think the ambulance would stop outside
her door? Ambulances take people to hospitals, not to
general practices in humdrum suburban streets. She
splashes her face with water from the tap and leans with
dripping face over the sink. And yet there was an instant,
a moment of madness, as the ambulance passed the
window and the lights flashed red against the waiting-
room wall, an instant when she believed that they — the
paramedics and their patient — were coming to find
her, to ask for her help. She would stand in the waiting
room, frozen with fear, as the patient died in front of
her, or she would bar the doorway and not let them in.

March 4

Sophie has just had a baby girl. 'Everything is great,' Sophie's husband, Hamish, tells her over the phone. 'We're going to call her Rosie. Wait until you see her. She's perfect.'

That evening they visit Sophie and the baby in hospital. Sophie is sitting by her bed having supper, devouring sandwiches in large bites and hastily gulping tea.

'Sorry to eat like a pig,' she says, wiping her mouth with the back of her hand, 'but she's going to wake any minute.'

Sophie's face is round and flushed, and there is a light film of sweat on her forehead. Her short, sleeveless nightdress does nothing to conceal the spread of her upper arms, her swollen feet and ankles. A layer of firm white fat encases her knees, and her thighs, pressed hard against the vinyl chair, are dimpled with cellulite. Leaning over to kiss Sophie, she sees, through the gaping flap of the maternity bra, the periphery of a dark brown areola, large and stark against the white, blue-veined skin of Sophie's breast.

It is time to see the baby. With a grunt Sophie eases herself out of the chair and lifts the swaddled infant from the crib. *Support her head*, she wants to say but stops herself.

'There, there, Rosie,' Sophie coos. She hooks her little finger through the baby's closed fist and regards them triumphantly. 'So, who wants the first hold?'

The baby is like all other newborns: red-faced and wrinkled, with oily, spotted skin, except that this baby also has a shock of black hair, a thicket of hair that stands straight on end. Comical, cartoonish hair—and so much of it. It will all fall out, soon enough. She takes the baby from Sophie and sits with her on the bed. William and Joe crowd around and stroke the baby's head.

'Why are you crying, Mum?' Joe asks her.

She tries to sound light-hearted. This is a happy occasion, after all. 'Women always cry when they hold newborn babies. It's just a silly thing women do.'

Paul, Hamish and the boys have gone to the kiosk and the baby is asleep on Sophie's breast. Most of the visitors have left and, save for the clatter of the medicine trolley on its evening round, the ward is quiet. From the window she looks down on the public gardens below, where the leaves of the elms have started to yellow. In the United States, she has heard, the autumn leaves are a tourist attraction, especially on the east coast, where, as the weather cools, the large deciduous forests of New England suddenly explode into colour; a great swathe of red and gold that moves southward, like a slow-burning forest fire, she imagines; a gradual migration of fall colour from the cold northern states to those of the milder south, the Carolinas and Virginia. She has heard that people from all over the world trek by their thousands to view this annual display. Such a journey could be pleasant, a comfortable pilgrimage in her old age: driving country roads through quaint New England towns; traversing the forests on foot, wrapped in a coat and a scarf against the gathering chill of the autumn afternoon.

The baby whimpers in Sophie's arms then quickly falls asleep again. 'Do you want to take her for a minute?' Sophie asks. 'Then she can go back in the crib.'

The infant is heavy with sleep; a warm, limp weight in her uncertain hands. How quickly one forgets how to cradle a newborn. How quickly one remembers.

'When I had William,' she finds herself saying, 'one of the midwives brought him into me a few hours after he was born and said, almost accusingly: "*This* baby needs a feed." I was worried that he'd been crying in the nursery while I'd been in bed, thinking about myself.' Yet here she is again, thinking of herself; talking about her experiences, now well in the past, while Sophie gave birth only yesterday.

Sophie stretches her legs along the bed, her swollen feet squeezed into pink sheepskin slippers. 'You'd had a difficult birth, remember. A sixteen-hour labour, or something horrific like that, then forceps, wasn't it? You would have needed a bit of time out.'

'Yes, maybe that's what it was.' It is kind of Sophie to

offer an excuse, although she does not deserve it. She sits in the armchair, still holding the baby, while Sophie takes up a magazine from the bedside table. On that first day, one of the midwives had shown her how to hold William when feeding. 'Make his head come to you,' she had said, her hand on the nape of William's neck. 'Don't lean the breast towards him or you'll end up with a sore back.' The midwife, a squat woman in her fifties, spoke of 'let-down' and 'attachment' and 'the breast' with a hard set to her mouth and a matter-of-factness reminiscent of sex-education classes at school, and she began to think of her own swollen breasts as attached only to William's puckered lips, no longer to the rest of her body.

After the midwife left she continued to sit as upright as she could in the bed, her hand supporting William's head as she had been shown, trying to visualise let-down: the surge of prolactin from her pituitary gland, the answering gush of milk from her nipples. She waited, too, for the flow of another sensation—a suffusion of bodily warmth or a pleasant, erotic tingling from head to foot, something to signal her newly found status—but instead her perineum ached and, despite the midwife's warning, she found herself leaning away from the pillows with shoulders hunched. The pull of William's mouth around her nipple became ever weaker and he was suddenly asleep, open-mouthed, his head slack in her cupped hand.

She sat still, unsure of what to do with a sleeping newborn, but before she even had time to cover her breast he was awake again and crying weakly. The skin around his neck hung loose, like that of an old man, and his tongue seemed dry and huge in his toothless mouth. She began to worry he was dehydrated or sick. Perhaps she was alert to something—an infection, a rare congenital disease— the midwives hadn't noticed. She stared, transfixed, at the sluggish movements of his tongue, backwards and forwards over his dry lips. His crying grew reassuringly stronger, built to an insistent wail and then a long exhaled crescendo of indignation: *Waaaaaaggghhhh*. Now she needed to silence him. But what should she do? It occurred to her, first vaguely and then with sudden clarity, that she must feed him. With her nipple in his mouth he could not cry. Her milk would content him, wouldn't it? He was her baby, hers to nourish, to clean, to placate, to please. For whom was she waiting? Only she could give him what he desired.

'The responsibility,' she says aloud, looking down at Rosie, still asleep in her arms. 'Try as they might, no one can explain it to you beforehand. But when it happens, the whole paradigm shifts. Nothing is ever the same again.'

Sophie drops her magazine to the floor. 'God, Anna, you make it all sound so heavy! How about some useful hints—you know, advice about nappy rash and cradle cap?' Sophie reaches for a bunch of grapes from the fruit bowl next to the bed. 'Anyway, the responsibility for Rosie isn't all mine. Hamish will have to do his share.'

She places the baby in the crib, folding and tucking the corners of the cotton blanket so that she is swaddled tight and warm. She runs her hand across Rosie's head and the thicket of black hair lies flat and soft against her palm. 'But there's something else, Sophie. In those three hours William had been in the nursery, out of my sight, I had forgotten he existed.'

That night in bed, Paul reaches out and touches her shoulder. 'Are you upset about the baby?'

'Upset? Why would I be upset?'

'You know why.'

'I'm happy for Sophie, happy for Hamish. Aren't you?'

'Anna, must I spell it out?'

'I don't know. You brought it up.'

'I don't want to make things harder for you by talking about it.'

'Talking about it? What more is there to say? It was an unplanned pregnancy. Unplanned and not entirely welcome.'

'You can't blame me for having doubts. We had never discussed having another child.'

'This is not about blame. I am simply stating the facts. I was pregnant then I miscarried. At nine weeks. Before you had made up your mind.'

'Anna—'

'It was a long time ago, now. Three years ago next month. All things considered, just a minor hiccup. Talking about it doesn't make things harder, but neither does it help.'

March 5

Margaret tells her that Joan Kennedy has phoned to request a home visit for her husband, Michael. He has run out of some of his medications. Could she possibly visit today?

She would like to tell Margaret to phone Joan straight back. *Tell her it is out of the question*, she wants to say. Joan, sprightly Joan, could easily drop by the clinic to pick up a script. But it is Michael, not Joan, with whom her duty lies. 'Please tell them I will be there today,' she tells Margaret. 'I can't promise what time.'

She inherited Michael Kennedy from the retiring doctor she replaced when she first joined the practice. Michael is fifty-eight years old, Irish-born, with longstanding diabetes. He was also once a smoker until his left leg was amputated above the knee: the fear of losing his right leg was incentive enough to give up cigarettes Michael has told her, on more than one occasion.

She goes to see him in her lunch break. Joan answers the door and ushers her, a firm hand on her back, through the narrow living room, along the passage and into Michael's room at the back of the house. He is there, as always, in his wheelchair, watching television, the screen so small that he must sit within an arm's reach of it.

'Michael, the doctor's here,' Joan says in her clipped brogue. 'Turn off the TV now and tell the doctor of all your complaints.' Joan waits until he has switched off the set and turned his chair, inching the wheels back and forth to face them. 'I'll leave you to it, then, Doctor,' she says briskly. A minute later, as is often the case when she visits, she hears Joan's car backing down the driveway.

She has never asked Michael where Joan goes on these occasions or why Joan always waits for her arrival before leaving the house, although it has occurred to her that Joan stays at home long enough to ensure the front door is opened when she knocks. But she does not believe Michael would intentionally refuse her entry. He treats her visits with a taciturn seriousness, producing for her inspection his dog-eared notebook of blood-sugar readings and a list of the medication he needs, all written in a slow, shaky hand; the drug names in uneven capitals, his numbers old-fashioned, his sevens crossed. He is always newly shaven and smelling of soap. She takes his blood pressure, listens to his chest, checks his pulse and the condition of the skin on his remaining foot. She writes prescriptions for insulin, anti-hypertensive medication and miscellaneous other things: a bottle of reagent strips, simple analgesics, the small dose of tricyclics he refers to as his 'sleepers'. There have been times, as Joan's car backs down the driveway, she has been on the verge of asking about the more secretive complications of his diabetes, but has always held back.

Michael would not take kindly to a woman meddling where she is not wanted.

His room is separated from the rest of the house by a covered walkway and a wooden ramp wide enough for a wheelchair to pass. The room contains a single bed, a wardrobe and a table on which the television stands. There are no photos, no books, save a weekly television guide. In the wardrobe, his medication bottles are lined neatly on a shelf and a single tweed jacket hangs from the rail. She would like to think that this spartan room is used only for her visits or as a daytime retreat: that, in the evenings, Michael turns off the television and enters the house proper, where he sits with Joan in the tiny living room, playing cards or backgammon, the gas heater blazing. She hopes, too, that after an evening's amusement, he sometimes finds warmth in Joan's double bed. Warmth and a woman's touch: his wife's soothing hand on the finely etched needle-marks scattered over his abdomen, on the withered skin of his stump.

On her way home from work she stops at the supermarket to buy something for dinner. As she returns to her car with the shopping a teenage boy on a skateboard flies past her, so close that she feels the vibration of the skateboard wheels through the concrete. She does not see the boy's face, yet — just for an instant — she thinks it is him, Ben Feltham, somehow whole again and wild with life.

It is not the first time this has happened. She often thinks she sees him somewhere — in a crowd, walking ten steps in front of her or crossing at the lights while she waits in her car. She knows of this phenomenon: the subconscious at work, projecting into consciousness the physical likeness of the one who occupies its nether realms, so that for a hallucinatory moment the conscious mind is convinced that its loved one has returned. Families of missing persons experience this often. But he is not her loved one—neither son, husband or brother; instead a patient whom she met just four times, and each time worse than the last. She has not laid eyes on him for three long years. By law she has been forbidden to see him. Would she have sought him out if she were free to? She might have followed him home, just once, at a distance, hiding in shadows, peering around corners, hoping to see him smile, to hear him laugh. If she could be reassured that, sometimes at least, he was happy.

In three years a boy can become a man, but still it is his seventeen-year-old self she sees on a street corner, or playing with his dog in the park. She hopes he has a dog, a loyal, doe-eyed animal who whines at the door when he is not there and sleeps on his bed at night. She sees him, this phantom boy, as he was at their first meeting: loose-limbed and awkward, his body, young for his years, not yet thickened and settled into adulthood. Seventeen: an awkward year in general, the odd year strung between the even sweetness of sixteen, and eighteen, the year of permission. What was she doing at seventeen? It is not a year she remembers well. He, on the other hand, will never forget it. *The year of cancer*, he will say. *The year of my amputation.*

March 6

Paul will not be going with her to mediation. She has asked him not to and he has agreed. This is the order in which things happened, although she finds herself recalling the sequence of events differently. Sometimes she catches herself thinking she asked him to accompany her but he refused.

'The prosecution's case rests entirely on your judgement about the need for an X-ray on that first or second visit,' John had explained at one of their early meetings. 'They are arguing on the grounds of delayed diagnosis. They'll have to crucify you to win and, believe me, they won't spare the nails.' She had imagined, then, the dramatics of the courtroom: a red-faced prosecuting barrister, gowned and wigged, sweeping through the chamber to point an accusatory finger at her, the wrong-doer, shivering in the dock. Mediation will be more comfortable, less gothic, John has assured her. A table and chairs; a private, carpeted room; no judges, wigs or gowns. Tea and coffee will be served. 'Even so,' John has said, 'their barrister will question your competence and credibility in no uncertain terms. His job, after all, is to further his client's interests, not yours. He will try to take you apart. It will not be easy for you.' So, despite the tea and coffee, she is not to be spared. But at least she can spare her husband.

But something about her request to Paul, and his acquiescence — perhaps, in retrospect, rather quickly obtained — still sits uneasily with her. She knows that, at some level, she is also shielding herself from his disappointment. Hasn't he always admired her for doing what she does? He has often listened to stories of her working day: her management of emergencies — the crushing chest pain of myocardial infarction, a sick, flaccid child in respiratory distress; her skills with a suture set; her willingness to delve into the labyrinthine workings of the human mind. She does not want him to see her professional behaviour being questioned, even ridiculed. She does not want him there when she falters, as she most certainly will.

When the writ was first served, such a long time ago, he had been painstakingly supportive of her; helping with the children's homework and the household chores, mowing the lawn on the weekends without being asked. But, in the last few weeks, as the date for mediation (marked in her diary, in red ink) draws ever closer, she has begun to sense an apprehension in him. Sometimes, when he looks at her across the dinner table, she catches the flicker of something like confusion on his face; as if, for an instant, the whole scene — his wife, his sons, the room in which they are seated — are completely unknown to him. *Jamais vu*: the disturbing strangeness of the familiar. She has tried to interpret this as anxiety for her, concealed because his role, in this situation at least, is to be strong, to downplay fear. But recently, as the back lawn grows longer and more unruly and he returns from work subdued, barely in time for dinner, she finds herself revising her initial diagnosis. Now, in her low moments, she looks at him across the table, sees the shadow again pass over his face and reads it as disappointment: that she could have come to this; that he could have come to this alongside her. At the eleventh hour, his belief in her has faltered: so she thinks now, when she is low.

Her practice partner, David Waldron, catches her between patients and asks to speak with her at lunchtime. She goes through the remainder of the morning with a vague uneasiness. What has she done? Has a patient complained? She was short with Margaret yesterday over a bungled telephone message. Has Margaret told David she is impossible to work with?

Margaret has been their receptionist for fifteen years. Every day she works wonders: soothing patients who arrive at the front desk angry or distressed, finding time for a sick child to be seen, remembering who is related to whom. When she was seven weeks pregnant with William, with bad morning sickness, it was Margaret who would greet her with a sweet cup of tea and a biscuit. Margaret was the first to guess her secret. And when her boys were born, Margaret knitted them each a jumper in pale baby wool: yellow for William, blue for Joe. She still has those jumpers, folded away in her baby drawer. It breaks her heart to think that Margaret might be angry with her.

At lunchtime she goes to David's room. He beckons her in and asks her to close the door behind her.

'There have been some phone calls, Margaret tells me,' he says.

'What sort of phone calls?'

'Someone phones and says nothing, just hangs up after a few seconds. Then they ring back, several times, over a half hour or so.'

She senses David is waiting for her opinion. 'It's probably just some kids making prank calls. William tells me it's a common pastime for some of the kids at school.' Could it in fact be William? He knows her work number.

'That's what Margaret thought, too, when it first started. But now it seems more'—he seems to be searching for the right word—'more intentional than that. And the calls are often in school hours, when it's unlikely a child could get to a phone.' He stresses *child* in such a way that she realises he doesn't think it is a child at all.

'And the caller never says anything?'

'Not a word.' He pauses. 'What do you think, Anna? What do you think we should do?'

'Do? What is there to do? Trace the calls, I suppose, if you're concerned about it. I can't say I am particularly worried.'

He fidgets with a pen then puts it back on his desk. 'Do you think … have you any reason to think it might have something to do with your court case? Have you had nuisance calls at home?'

She laughs to cover her irritation. Must everything come back to her? 'No, David, nothing so sinister. I think you're reading too much into this. It's just some kids, or a few wrong numbers. It will stop, sooner or later.'

-56-

March 8

They have rented a house on the west coast for the Labour Day weekend. It is the end of summer, but she does not mind. She sees herself now as more attuned to the patterns of autumn: the cool undercurrents of even the sunniest days, the nights closing in, crisp and still. She knows Paul will grieve the end of the hot weather.

They set out early Saturday morning, the station wagon packed tightly with suitcases and boxes of food—good bread, fresh fruit, Paul's favourite muesli—the bodyboards wedged into the spaces between. From the city they drive for an hour and a half, through brown-brick suburbs that reluctantly give way to flat, denuded farmland. The boys, unused to the rhythm of long car trips, niggle at each other in the back seat. From time to time she turns to stare hard at them, her finger to her lips. As they near the coast the road begins to rise, then suddenly emerges through the trees so that they are at cliff height, overlooking the ocean, the sun bright in their eyes. 'There's the lighthouse!' William says, pointing ahead and, yes, there it is, marooned on its solitary outcrop, iconic and somehow cheerfully desolate, the tower pristinely white, the dome too red, its round windows winking in the sunlight.

'Do you remember it from the last time we were here?' she asks.

'I don't know. I remember it from somewhere.'

They stop for milk at the general store. There is a small café next to the store: a lean-to construction, brightly painted with a new timber deck at the front. 'Let's have a drink,' she suggests. She orders coffees and a milkshake each for the boys and they sit together at an outside table. It seems quiet for a holiday weekend but it is still early: the place will be busy by lunchtime. The boys, too, are quiet, concentrating on their drinks, their cheeks concave with sucking. After this they will want to go to the beach right away. Tomorrow, if it is too cool for swimming, they might all go for a walk in the hinterland. The morning after that, against Paul's advice, she will bundle the boys outside and clean the house. They will manage a last trip to the beach and a hurried lunch of leftovers before packing the car to go home. Already she sees herself back at work, driving into the car park on Tuesday morning, leaning her head against the car window for a few seconds, her eyes closed — if she were of a religious bent she might see this eye-closing, this moment of silence as a prayer for composure — before entering the clinic, a full day's work ahead of her.

With a growing irritation she sips her coffee, trying to extract from the act the pleasure she knows must be there, if only she would allow herself to feel it. She must try harder to live in the moment, to savour the here and now, the taste of the coffee—even though it is a little weak—the sun on her back. If she could sit with the autumn sun always on her back, perhaps she would do better. But, even as she urges herself to do so, she knows that part of her rebels against the philosophy of the here and now, the concentration on the sensory present that she finds too concrete, almost animal in its simplicity. The capacity to project, to plan, to anticipate and, yes, to worry about the future: aren't such abstractions evidence of a higher-level thinking? Why should she relinquish all this for the mundane pleasure of the moment?

The boys are sucking hard on their straws, draining the last of their milkshakes while Paul reads the newspaper, seemingly oblivious to the noise. 'Don't slurp,' she tells the boys. 'Stop slurping *now*, or I'll take your straws away.'

After lunch, they walk to the nearest swimming beach. It is low tide and the air is languidly warm, even humid. The boys take their bodyboards into the water and Paul follows. Sitting on a towel, she watches them. William, turned to shore, looks back over his shoulder for the next wave to catch, while Joe, closer to shore but facing out to sea, is tossed and tipped at random by the shore break. Paul stands in the shallows, arms folded, legs apart. He wades over to William and positions him to catch a wave, pushing William's board forward as the wave swells behind him. In his board shorts Paul looks lean, his back and arms strong. Perhaps he has lost a little weight. He is a good father, a good man: all in all, an attractive man. In earlier times this would have been a satisfying thought. She opens her book and begins to read.

When, some ten minutes later, she looks up she sees Paul talking to a couple with a large dog on a lead. She does not recognise the couple, who seem, from a distance, to be young and athletic. Joe leaves the water and, discarding his board on the sand, runs up to the dog and pats it. The woman bends down, kneeling by the dog, her hand on its collar, and talks to Joe. That woman does not have children, she thinks. She returns to reading, only putting down her book when Paul and the boys come back.

'Who were those people?' She wonders if she sounds accusatory.

'Kate Devine and Nick, her boyfriend, I suppose. Kate is one of our designers. I must have mentioned her before.'

'Maybe. I can't remember.'

Paul rubs his body vigorously with a towel. He shakes the water from his hair and a shower of fine droplets spatters her face and shoulders. 'They're staying close by. I've invited them over for a drink this evening.'

'I see.' She is all at once despondent, feeling Paul's enthusiasm for extra company as a pointed criticism of her own. She wipes her face with the edge of her towel.

'Don't worry,' Paul says. 'You won't need to do anything.'

They are, the four of them, sitting on the deck, drinking wine. The introductions have all been made, and Paul has given his guests a quick tour of the house. She has arranged dips and crackers on a plate and put the insect repellent within easy reach. The boys are inside, watching a DVD. All that now remains is to sit and talk to Nick and Kate, these two strangers, with whom she already knows she is unlikely to find a connection. She has grown unused to it, this making of conversation for conversation's sake, this proximity to people who *do not understand*. For three years, more or less, she has avoided such situations. And now, unexpectedly, here she is, sitting on this beach-house deck on this warm, somewhat exotic night, listening to Nick talk about sport—about triathlons in particular. Nick appears to know a great deal about triathlons. As he talks she thinks of the beach on which she spent the afternoon, trying to picture it in the waning light. There might still be people down there: fishermen casting their lines from the rocks; love-struck adolescents who, having escaped from the family barbecue, are now lying together in the dunes, the sand shifting and sifting beneath them — now cool, now warm—as they awkwardly fondle and undress.

'I'll just get the boys something to eat,' she says, after Nick has finished yet another anecdote, the point of which she has again failed to grasp. 'Please excuse me for a moment.'

From the kitchen window she looks out onto the deck. Nick has moved his chair closer to Kate and Paul, and the three of them are in conversation together. Both men are turned towards Kate, who sits between them, legs outstretched, ankles crossed, talking and laughing. When Kate first arrived, fresh and smiling, her hair drawn back, she noticed, among other things, a silver chain around her left ankle, fringed with silver leaves that shimmered as she walked. The shimmering drew one's attention, perhaps deliberately so, to Kate's delicate ankles and her high, slender calves. Kate has the type of legs she has always viewed—along with long fingers and large breasts, both of which she has noticed Kate also possesses—as a sign of aristocratic breeding. An absurd notion, really: a sort of warped eugenic thinking. She would never mention it to anyone. She peels a carrot and cuts it into strips.

With an exuberant laugh, Kate begins a story about one of the firm's more notorious clients: a wealthy older man, eccentric, obsessive. She has heard Paul tell such stories in the past. As Kate talks, she rocks back on the legs of her chair, extending her arms behind her to hold the deck railings. As if there is an invisible string from her body to theirs, both Nick and Paul lean slightly towards her as she leans back. Nick puts his large hand on her thigh. Kate's story progresses in fits and starts, punctuated with laughter and exclamations from both of the men. From time to time Paul interrupts Kate, embellishing her tale, turning it around, making it his own. Kate looks at him benignly, sweetly as he talks; she has a pretty face, an open face. She could only be in her late twenties, at most. Through the open window she hears the animation in Paul's voice and recognises it as foreign: a new thing from a new place. That woman has the ability to make men happy, she thinks. She stays in the kitchen, busying herself with the children's dinner. It seems she is not missed.

It is the middle of the night when Paul wakes her with his hand on her breast, his mouth on her mouth. He seems half asleep. His breath is stale with alcohol, but she does not push him away, instead she wriggles herself underneath him in readiness. He enters her immediately, moving quickly and forcefully in a rhythm of his own, one hand pawing at her breast, then brushing against her face. He has the groping hands of a blind man. Lust, she says to herself in the dark, lust that is not meant for me. Still, it is not without its rewards. She feels the passion even so, feels the tingle of desire pass through his body to hers. He comes with a short cry, his neck arched, his face turned towards the ceiling. He does not speak. Within thirty seconds he is asleep again. She stays awake, her back to him, her knees bent to her chest, nursing to herself a hard kernel of something that feels too satisfying to be indignation.

March 14

She has never worried about her looks before. Never worried, perhaps, because in the past she has never had to, being young or at least youngish, and, while not beautiful, having no obvious physical detractions. Now, at forty-three, she feels she has missed the chance to make the most of herself. Her philosophy has always been to make the most of herself in other ways: in her studies and her profession, in the kind of books she reads and the films she sees. She has always sought fulfilment in matters of the intellect, rather than in grooming. There has never seemed to be enough time for both, the grooming and the intellect, the attention to both body and mind, but it could be that she has never seen it as important to make the time. Maybe lack of time is not the real reason for her ignorance of cosmetics, her meagre jewellery collection.

When she sees herself, now, in unfamiliar mirrors, when she catches her reflection in shop windows, she is shocked by how she looks: her skin dull, leached of colour, the general drawing-down of her face now that her skin, having resisted forty years of gravitational pull, has finally given up the fight. It is as if she is seeing someone else looking back at her with a slightly hostile expression, someone vaguely familiar whom she cannot quite place. From her university lectures, she recalls the histology of ageing skin: the gradual depletion of elastin, the degeneration of collagen, the decreasing ability of older skin to hold water in its deeper layers. (How aware she is of the freshness of young skin, bursting with water, the underlying dermis so plump and resilient. Skin like that of a ripe, round, juicy peach! These days she takes a voyeuristic pleasure in the bloom on the skin of young women.) She has come to resent this biochemical knowledge, instilled in her years ago, when she dutifully copied down the lecturer's words, never thinking how her own skin would one day grow loose and thin and dry. (If only she had not spent so much time in the sun, lying on her back, her face and neck bare, unshaded, her eyes squinting against the glare—the crow's feet, the solar keratoses she cultivated in her twenties.) Having absorbed such knowledge at an impressionable age, she now finds it difficult to discount. These days, when she looks in the mirror, she wishes she knew less about her ageing body. She would rather not know what is to come.

While out shopping for children's socks in her lunch break she passes a beauty salon. On an impulse she decides to go in. A doorbell sounds as she enters and a young woman in a white tunic and pants appears from the back of the shop.

'Can I help you?' she asks with a slight inclination of her head.

The girl's face is expertly made-up: foundation of a salmon-pink hue, the faintest hint of blusher along her cheekbones, lip gloss and eyeliner impeccably applied. Her hair is pulled, sleek and tight, away from her face. The effect is somewhat intimidating.

'I'd like something for my face, please. A moisturiser.'

The young woman scans her face with a critical eye. 'What are you using at present?'

'Just something I bought at the supermarket. I'm not sure of the brand.'

The girl raises her eyebrows. She might have guessed that supermarket cosmetics would not meet with her approval. 'Have you ever used our products before?' the young woman asks, sounding sceptical. She beckons with a manicured finger over to a glass-shelved cabinet. 'I'd suggest a cleanser and a moisturiser. And a neck cream at night.'

Instinctively her hands go to her throat. She has never before considered her neck in need of attention. Has it already come to that?

The young woman—does she call herself a beautician, or is that an outdated term?—selects three different-sized boxes from the cabinet and takes them to the counter, where she opens each with her long, shiny nails. 'An excellent night-time cleanser,' she says, offering the first jar for her inspection, 'and a rich moisturiser, suitable for your type of skin.'

'My type of skin? And what is that?'

The girl does not hesitate. 'Mature skin. This is designed for delicate, more mature skin.'

The diagnosis has been made, the treatment dispensed, and all so promptly.

'Fine,' she says, business-like, taking her credit card from her wallet and holding it up between finger and thumb. 'I'll take the lot.'

A minute later she is in the street again, clutching her little blue-and-white carry bag of purchases, for which she has just paid the ridiculous sum of one hundred and fifty dollars. Why did she do it? She could have declined the young woman's lukewarm offer of a twenty-dollar discount on all three items and left the salon with her wallet still intact, if not her pride. Instead she signed the credit slip with an extra flourish and let the door slam on her way out. She shoves the purchases into her shoulder bag and zips it closed: she does not want Margaret to see her parading through the waiting room with a bag of expensive cosmetics. Is it too late to return them? A moment's embarrassment: that is all it would cost her. She need never visit that salon again.

But it is time to return to work. She starts to walk in the direction of the clinic and with each step her irritation increases. She will keep the cosmetics, but not because she believes they will help her ageing skin or, for that matter, help in any other way: together they constitute neither active treatment nor placebo. They are simply an admission—these fragrant creams in their opaque glass jars, these snake-oil elixirs of youth—an admission that she (despite her scepticism, her knowledge of histology,

her years of devotion to cruel, hard fact) is as vain and
foolish as any other woman of her age.

She is in the bath. She has locked the bathroom door.
The water, still warm, gently laps against her thighs and
over her stomach. Leaning back against the edge of the
bath she idly regards the length of her body. For someone
who spends so much of her time in the examination of
naked flesh, it is strange that she rarely gives her own
body more than a cursory glance. She is naked now and,
at this minute, in no particular hurry: what better time to
take stock of herself? Time to look at her breasts, at the
flattening of the upper curvature, the smattering of dark
hairs around each nipple. Beneath her breasts the skin of
her abdomen, softly crinkled and loose from pregnancy,
is strung like a hammock between the two iliac spines.
And then, the convexity of her hips and outer thighs: how
preserved the skin is there, how white and smooth. If only
she had always stayed out of the sun! She looks along the
curved line of the quadriceps muscle to the knees with
their bony patellae, the soft flesh of their inner borders.
This is her body: no more, no less. The ordinary body
of a forty-three-year-old woman, weathered, perhaps, a
little more than most. Is this how other people see her?

She turns onto her right side, her legs bent, and
notices how the refraction of the water's surface makes it
look, from her angle of sight, as if her left leg is separated,
mid-calf, from the rest of her body. The longer she lies
in this position, the easier it is to believe. She stares at

her left foot until its very appearance becomes grotesque, like a plaster fake that has somehow ended up in this bath beside her. A clean, painless cleaving: would that it were always so. The water is getting cold and Joe is knocking on the bathroom door, calling to her.

March 22

On Saturday morning she takes Joe to his drama class in South Yarra. They are running late, so she drops him at the theatre then drives around the neighbouring streets until she finds somewhere to park. She turns off the engine and sits for a while. The sun through the windows gently heats the car interior so that it feels pleasantly lazy to sit, doing nothing. As she begins to drift off to sleep, a thought comes to her from nowhere: she has wasted her opportunities, wasted the opportunity to live not a better life, but a safer one. A safer, more comfortable life: that is what she wants. If she had chosen more wisely along the way — law, perhaps, or commerce, instead of medicine; plastic surgery instead of general practice; long, lustrous hair instead of a short cropped style that probably makes her face look too thin — she might, at this exact moment, be buying her weekly flowers from the florist at the end of this street in preparation for her dinner guests, instead of sitting here, alone in her car, uselessly thinking. Perhaps it is just the sun through the window, or the eerie quiet of the street in which she waits, but she has a sudden dislocating sense of all things crystallising, the events of her life overlapping and aligning so that a pattern emerges, a pattern of choices that has led her, inexorably, to this moment of reckoning.

She shakes herself awake, out of her reverie. She has always been prone to reflection on days such as this—the autumn sunshine, the sky, at late morning, cloudless and blue, yet the air still cool. Autumn is always a time for reflection. A gentle southerly breeze wafts perfectly, so that as she lowers the window she feels the cool air on her face, curing her drowsiness but leaving her feeling as if she has just awoken from a deep sleep, unsure of her surroundings. It is this street, too, that has set her thinking: this tram-tracked street of Victorian terraces and lush front gardens where palms sway stiffly and red begonias bloom on upstairs balconies; where, around the corner at an expensive café opposite the gardens, she will soon sit and drink coffee while she skims the Saturday newspapers. This understated wealth, the gentility of this suburb unsettles her so that she begins to think of choices and consequences, of having and forgoing, of never wanting in the first place but, perhaps later, when looking at the red flowers on an upstairs balcony, of coming to regret one's youthful resolve.

From inside the car she watches two men standing on the pavement. They are inspecting the car parked in front of her—a black Alfa Romeo, sleek and new. The older man is doing most of the inspecting, walking around the car and taking photos of it from different angles. The younger man lifts the bonnet and her view of them both is obscured. She imagines them leaning over the engine and fiddling with caps and bolts like excited schoolboys. The bonnet is set down with a gentle clang. The men return to the pavement and continue talking, their eyes still on the car as though it might vanish should they let it out of their sight. The negotiation, if that is what it is, appears to be going well. The older man smiles and strokes his neat, white beard as he listens to his companion. Occasionally they both break into restrained laughter.

The older one is dressed as if ready for work, in a pale pink business shirt, a tie and belted trousers. A daring colour, pink, for a man in his fifties, which he appears to be. He has a pleasant face, wide and smooth above his beard. Through the open car window she thinks she hears a Scottish accent, a soft, refined Scottish brogue carried to her on the breeze that ruffles the bearded man's hair and rustles the leaves of the garden palms. She wonders if he lives nearby. Having come here, perhaps, from the cobblestoned streets of Edinburgh, he might find a small remnant of home in this leafy suburb, with its cafés and bookshops, its claims to a dignified history.

The two men shake hands: it seems the negotiation is complete, at least for the moment. The older man gives the younger one his card. He then crosses the street and turns the corner, a spring in his step. She imagines him going home to his wife to tell her of his purchase. *You and your cars*, his wife might say, kissing him on his cheek, her top lip brushing the smooth skin above his beard, and she is again brought to thinking of choices and consequences, of the possibility of lives other than the one she is living.

April 2

In the practice of medicine most things are arbitrary. This is what she tells herself as she climbs the wheel-chair ramp each morning, and again in the waiting room where, every time she enters, a dozen expectant faces turn towards her. *Most things are arbitrary*: she should tattoo it on her wrist.

Of course there are still some absolutes: it is wrong to intentionally harm a patient, for instance. In most circumstances, but not all, it is wrong to break confidentiality. It is always wrong to enter into a sexual relationship with a patient. But for the rest, the day-to-day interactions, it seems to her now to be more an issue of style than of substance. Whether to review a patient in one day or two, to order investigations immediately or at the next visit: such decisions she used to make in a considered manner, as if she were able to judge from some sort of elevated position, looking down at all the facts, the risks and benefits, the full stretch of medical knowledge laid out beneath her, to come to some sort of absolute decision, the *right* decision, about her patient's care. Now she sees, with startling clarity, that these decisions were not right, but relative.

In medical school, in first-year sociology, she was taught about the relativity of medical treatment, at least with respect to the patient. A doctor's management, the lecturer had said, must take into account the patient's individual circumstances. Treatments should be tailor-made to fit the old and the young, the poor and the rich; culture, gender and beliefs must be respected and catered for. She has known all this for a long time. But until now she had always thought herself a constant in the doctor–patient equation.

This new relativity she has discovered is in regards to herself in the role of doctor: a role she plays with less and less conviction. Her past experiences; her irrational, at times subconscious fears; her feelings about the patient before her; the time of the day—evening clinic is always more anxiety-provoking, she can admit that now; her level of fatigue: these things and countless others, the antitheses of reason and factual knowledge, insinuate themselves into her rational, conscious decision-making process, so that what she produces is not the right decision in any absolute sense but, instead, an arbitrary compromise, hurriedly patched together from a thousand shadowy, niggling impulses.

If her decisions are arbitrary, they are less valuable than she had previously thought. Her decisions, being arbitrary, must therefore lack conviction. Doesn't conviction imply a belief in the absolute? She no longer believes in the absolute, nor in absolution.

On her afternoon off she visits Sophie with some food —an orange cake, bought from the bakery, and some homemade soup. She is careful to knock quietly at the front door, in case they are sleeping.

Sophie answers the door, still in her dressing-gown, the baby squirming on her shoulder. 'Thank God you've come. Now I can have a shower.' She follows Sophie into the kitchen and places the cake on the bench, the soup in the refrigerator. Sophie hands her the baby. 'She's been so unsettled this morning. I've hardly been able to get to the bathroom.'

'Have your shower now, and I'll try to get her to sleep.' She feels as if she is speaking to a child. She carries Rosie into the bedroom and lays her on the change table. Rosie starts to cry. 'There, there,' she sings. 'It will all be over in a minute.' She undoes the disposable nappy and checks it for dampness. It seems completely dry, so different from those flimsy towelling nappies she used for her babies: the two-hourly changing, the cheap plastic pants that split and tore, the inevitable nappy rash. But, when she thinks of the billions of disposable nappies now lying in landfill all over the planet, she does not regret the inconvenience. She does not even regret the nappy rash her sons had to endure: surely everyone, even babies, must suffer a little for the sake of a greater good? *Suffer the little children.* She would like to think she has brought up her sons to consider the greater good.

She places Rosie, still fretting, in the cot, then finds a cotton blanket and swaddles her firmly. Attached to the head of the cot is a pull-ring toy clown. She pulls the cord and the clown dances to a music-box version of Brahm's lullaby. Rosie stops crying and lies still; she is listening to the music. Maybe she will sleep, after all. She leans against the side of the cot and waits until the music stops, then pulls the cord once more. She does not remember waiting by the cot for her sons to fall asleep but then she, too, would have been impatient to escape to the bathroom or the phone. Besides, her sons would have sensed her there, hovering over them, would have smelled her milk, the particular scent of her body and would have cried to be picked up and fed. But Rosie does not demand this of her. She watches as the baby's eyes close, while the lullaby slows then peters out.

While Rosie sleeps, she and Sophie sit in the kitchen, drinking coffee and eating cake. The house is quiet and warm. Sophie's hair, still damp from the shower, is starting to curl in wisps around her face. Two small circular patches of milk have seeped through the front of her T-shirt.

'Do you want another baby?' Sophie asks.

How can she begin to answer? 'I'm almost forty-three.'

'So? You know it's still possible. Do you want another baby or not?'

'It's complicated, Sophie.'

'No, it's not. It's actually very simple.'

A memory comes to her: that of Sophie as a thirteen-year-old, standing in the kitchen, nagging for new clothes as her mother chops carrots for dinner. 'My friends get more clothes in a month than I get in a year,' Sophie complains.

'Maybe your friends have more money than we do,' she chimes in from the family room, where she is studying at the table. 'Maybe your friends are just spoiled.'

Sophie gives her a withering glance, then turns her attention back to her mother. 'It's not fair,' she whines, over and over, to be stopped only by her mother's soft, defeated cry of pain as the vegetable knife slices cleanly through her finger. Red-faced with indignation, the quick-burning indignation of an older sister, she strides into the kitchen and slaps Sophie across the face. 'You stupid, selfish bitch! Now look what you've done.' She sees herself wrapping a clean tea towel around her mother's bloody finger while Sophie stands rigid, wide-eyed, her hand to her smarting cheek.

She tells her patients who ask that the chance of miscarriage is one in five. She has heard other figures used—one in four, one in six—nevertheless she sticks with one in five because she believes the concept of risk, in this case at least, to be slippery, evanescent; like a shining fish in a stream, never to be caught and held in one's hand. Does it matter to the woman who miscarries if the risk was one in five or one in a thousand? Despite all the statistics in the world, her loss remains her loss: a private thing, essentially immeasurable. A loss of part of herself, in a way. As to how much of oneself is likely to be lost, there is no ready calculation at hand. To the pregnant woman who does not ask, she says nothing of risk. Why spoil her excitement? There will be time enough to be anxious later on.

A woman called Emma comes to see her. She confirmed Emma's pregnancy just three weeks ago: a happy occasion, as far as she can recall. Today Emma looks worried.

'How are things going?' she asks. She smiles expectantly but is careful to keep her question general.

'I am bleeding,' Emma answers.

She tries to organise an ultrasound. She phones the local imaging centres but cannot get Emma an appointment that day. 'You will need to go to the women's hospital,' she tells her. 'They will do an ultrasound there. I will write you a letter to take with you.'

'Does this mean I will lose the baby?' Emma asks.

'Perhaps.'

'Is there anything that can be done to save it?'

'No, nothing. I'm sorry.'

She sees Emma again, three days later. Emma has miscarried. Crying, Emma tells the story: how her bleeding and pain increased after she got to the hospital, how her husband steadied her by holding her hand during the ultrasound examination. She had lain on the bed, straining to interpret what she saw on the monitor as the doctor moved the probe back and forth across her skin. Try as she might, she could make no sense of the shifting grey shapes she saw on the screen. 'Where is my baby?' she asked the doctor. Emma tells of the shaking of the doctor's head, of his final words before he left the room: 'I'm sorry, but we cannot find a beating heart.' Does Emma worry that, in some dark corner of her womb, unseen by medical eyes, a tiny heart still lies feebly beating?

Emma wants to go over events leading up to the miscarriage, although nothing may have led to it in a causative sense. *These things just happen*, she could say to Emma and she would be right. But surely something or someone must be to blame. Emma wants to examine the time of conception. 'Was I drinking too much? Did I have a vitamin deficiency?' Emma wonders aloud. How far back should Emma go? How much of her past should she lay open to scrutiny? If Emma is to search for all possible answers, she must start at the beginning, at her own conception. 'Did I overexert myself, or work too hard?' Emma asks. 'Was it right to have sex so early in the pregnancy?' She is worried that, during climax, the shudders of her womb have shaken her foetus from its moorings. 'Should I have abstained from intercourse, deferred my gratification for the sake of my baby?' Emma wants to know. The answer is no and yes. While she can reassure Emma on the question of sex, the answer to the larger question is yes: of course a woman's pleasure must be deferred for the sake of her child.

Blood and pain, hallmarks of illness and injury: the former seen and measured in millilitres; the latter only felt and therefore, in medical terms, a lesser symptom. Better, perhaps, for a woman to bleed by the bucketful and feel nothing at all. And yet the pain of a miscarriage: one could strap a monitor to a woman's abdomen and observe the tiniest of blips as the uterine muscle barely flickers. Nothing like the fierce contractions of labour, yet a hundred times worse. Blood and pain and absence: a hollowing out, when all she yearns for is fullness and presence.

'Do you have children?' Emma asks through her tears. She asks because she needs to know if her doctor truly understands. If she must share her secret with someone, then let it be someone with children. She might better ask of her doctor: *Have you ever had a miscarriage?* But it is unlikely Emma will go that far. Talk of children is sunny, open and wholesome; miscarriages are whispered about in airless, dark places. Now that Emma has been to that place, she will not expect others to follow.

'Yes, I have children,' she replies. She does not say she has miscarried, too.

April 11

William's teacher, Mrs Hammond, sends her an email, asking to speak with her *about William's general behaviour*. She is surprised by this: William's behaviour, both at home and school, has never been an issue before. She meets with the teacher the following afternoon. They sit in the classroom on the children's blue plastic chairs, low to the ground. The room is a mess, the bookcases crammed and untidy, the rubbish bin overflowing with paper. On the floor, underneath the blackboard, workbooks teeter in a ragged pile.

'William is a lovely boy,' Mrs Hammond begins. 'Focused, considerate of the other children—but you probably already know this.' She clears her throat, adjusts her glasses. 'It's just that lately I've noticed a change in him.'

'In what way?'

'He's more distracted. He doesn't volunteer answers any more, he's not as careful about his work. And there was an incident in the playground last Friday. It's difficult to know exactly what happened—William and the other boy involved have conflicting stories.'

'Will didn't say anything to me about it. Was he hurt?'

'He was upset, crying, but no, he hadn't been hurt physically. I wanted to call you—he seemed quite distressed—but he said he didn't want to bother you at work. He was quite adamant about it.' Mrs Hammond looks at her pointedly.

'I don't know why he would say that.'

'I suspect he was trying to protect you from something,' the teacher says, shifting in her seat.

So this is what it's about, this little tête-à-tête. Using my son to get to me, to get at me. 'I don't know what you mean,' she says coldly.

'My impression is that something was said in the playground—something unkind—and William reacted.'

'Something unkind?'

Mrs Hammond looks uncomfortable. 'Something about you, in particular.'

She suddenly understands. 'About my court case, do you mean?'

'Yes, I'm afraid so.'

It has followed me here, to this children's playground, and found my son. She feels the blood drain from her face. As surreptitiously as she can, she grips the edge of the seat with both hands to steady herself. But surely she could have predicted this. If she had been thinking clearly, *thinking of her son instead of herself*, she might have taken preventive action. The trial has been in all the newspapers, will have been discussed at the dinner table of many a family in the neighbourhood. Everyone—those who know her well, even those who know her only well enough to greet her briefly at the school fence, or point her out to others when her back is turned—will feel entitled to their opinion. And of course they *are* entitled: it is a public matter, a civil matter, after all—though a shiver travels along her spine when she thinks of her name spoken, her actions dissected by those who stand behind her in the supermarket queue. If she put her ear to the pavements of this suburb, would she hear the whispering? As she walks her children home from school do the telephone wires above her hum with her name? She can easily imagine what children might make of those overheard conversations: *someone's leg was cut off*. They probably have her wielding the saw. *Your mother cut off a boy's leg*: that is how William would have heard it. *My dad says she is a bad doctor. A witch doctor*, perhaps: do children know of such things these days? *She pretends she's a doctor but she's really a witch*.

'Who was it?' she asks. 'Who said this to William?'

Mrs Hammond sighs and names the child. 'Please remember, we don't know exactly what happened. I've already spoken to the boy, given him a warning. Maybe we should leave it there, for William's sake.'

Mrs Hammond is right. She recognises the boy's name. He is one of the school troublemakers: not the sort of child who will respond well to punishment, much less an appeal to his better instincts. Although, at this moment, she wants to grab the boy by the arm—*by the scruff of his neck and push him up against a wall*—it will be better for William, better for her, too, that she plays the incident down. *It's not fair*, she wants to protest to Mrs Hammond, who sits there, watching her over her glasses, her ample hips squeezed into the ridiculously small chair. She wants to stride across the room, throw open the window and shout across the empty asphalted yard: *Leave my son alone. It has nothing to do with him.*

There is a knock at the classroom door. She turns to see Joe at the window, smiling impishly. Behind him stands William, white-faced, anxious. She nods and tries to smile reassuringly but he scowls at her and turns away. Does he know what this meeting is about? He has not asked why she was coming in today, but of course that means nothing. *He is only ten years old.* She is washed out, close to tears. *My eldest son, my defender. My poor little boy.*

'I must go. The boys have swimming lessons now.' She stands, stiffly. Her legs feel lifeless, unstable. 'I'll speak to William tonight about … everything. Thank you for letting me know.'

'He's a lovely boy,' Mrs Hammond says again, standing, too, and smoothing her skirt. She waves through the glass at William. He does not wave back. 'A sensitive, intelligent boy. I wanted to mention: we have a school psychologist who visits once a week—if you wanted William to see her.'

She bristles. 'See her? For counselling, you mean? I'm not sure that's needed at this point.'

Mrs Hammond stands her ground. 'I understand it's been a difficult time—for you and your family. Whatever we can do to help.' She pauses expectantly, her face composed into an earnest, enquiring expression. *Let's get to the bottom of this*, her expression reads. *Let's get things out in the open, shall we?* Enquiring or inquisitive?

Do not use your teacherly ways on me, she thinks. *Do not patronise me*. 'I appreciate your concern,' she answers, as if to end the matter, 'but I am sure we can manage.' She starts to move away, afraid that Mrs Hammond might put a hand on her arm or, worse still, attempt to hug her.

At the door she turns back. 'Just for future reference, I am always—have always been—happy for the school to contact me at work. I would never …' She trails off. Whatever it was she was about to say—she is not quite sure herself—she cannot finish. She shrugs her shoulders and leaves, closing the door behind her.

April 14

Sophie tells her that she has consulted a naturopath for a breastfeeding problem. The naturopath has diagnosed the condition as candidiasis. 'If she can't fix it I will have to stop breastfeeding,' Sophie says. 'The pain is driving me crazy.'

She is surprised, even a little insulted, that Sophie has not asked her advice. Of course she does not want to treat her sister. Nevertheless, she might have advised her in general terms. Instead Sophie has transferred her problem from one paradigm to another, from Western medicine to that of alternative health. She understands that this is happening all the time, that many of her own patients also consult alternative health practitioners, that the complementary health industry is burgeoning —but that *her sister* would see a naturopath *instead of* a GP.

When she graduated from medical school, Sophie, then seventeen, gave her a boxed coffee mug decorated with the words: *Congratulations! You've made it!* The next year, during her country-hospital rotation, Sophie travelled by train to stay for a week in her poky hospital flat. Doesn't Sophie remember those nights she was on call? Didn't Sophie stir at the sound of the telephone, wake just long enough to glance at the clock each time she left her bed to go to the wards? The things she did on those wards at night. She had been a doctor for only six months. During the week Sophie stayed she performed a lumbar puncture, her first unsupervised, on a febrile infant who had just had a seizure. The emergency-room nurse held the small body still, tucking the child's head into his drawn-up knees so that the tiny vertebrae, like knuckles, curved out towards her. The old man with terminal heart failure whose stuttering, suffocating death she intruded upon each time she entered his room to give him a little more morphine. A little more, no more. He had once been the town mayor. His son, the local policeman, had cried at the bedside as he held his dead father's hand. Over breakfast, didn't she tell Sophie of her nocturnal duties? But perhaps she had been too tired to talk. Perhaps Sophie had not been ready to listen.

Sophie argues that GPs do not give her enough time. She tells Sophie to stop visiting extended-hours, bulk-billing clinics where inexperienced doctors are under pressure to push patients through. Really, she is annoyed by Sophie's double standards. While her sister complains about the quality of care she receives from a bulk-billing clinic, she is willing to pay for a forty-minute consultation with a naturopath. It is more and more a case of attaching value to something one has paid for and devaluing something one receives for *free*.

For five years before joining David and Rohan, she

worked in a community health centre in a working-class area of the city. One evening a week, as part of her job, she saw patients at an outreach clinic; a converted shopfront in a down-at-heel shopping strip where the streetlights were often broken and the walls were splattered with graffiti of an artless and angry kind. Most of the time spent there she patched up social problems: drug use, alcoholism, depression—the ravages of long-term unemployment. Being a salaried government employee, she knew nothing of the costs of providing care: all she need do was ensure that each patient signed their Medicare form. Whether patients valued their care or not was all one to her then.

It is only since entering private practice in a more affluent suburb that she has begun to question her value. Despite the given wisdom that all patients deserve equal access and equal care—and philosophically, intellectually she adheres to this—she realises she makes a distinction between those who pay and those who do not. It is not rewarding, rather it is burdensome to see paying patients. She feels an extra pressure to perform, to provide *value*, once money has entered the equation. She spends longer with these patients, longer than she should, sits acquiescent as they bring out their checklists, and still feels she has not done enough. She is especially uncomfortable with seeing the children of paying parents, these children in their private-school uniforms who regard her coolly, who, she imagines, are asked by their parent on exiting the clinic: *Did you like that doctor? Should we go back to her?*

The concept of general practice as small business sits uneasily with her; that her skills are a commodity to which a monetary value is attached still seems, after eleven years in private practice, a little grubby. Paul has told her to be realistic. She is providing a valuable service and that, after all those years of medical training, she should in fact be charging more. And when the dishwasher repairman arrives at the house, demanding, somewhat rudely, a hundred dollars to set foot in the door, she can see Paul's point. She cannot help but compare the service provided by the dishwasher repairman to that which she provides. Though, it must be said, the dishwasher man will leave with the dishwasher fixed, in running order. When it comes to her patients, she cannot always make such a claim.

The government pays her fifty-three dollars for a standard home visit; eighty-two for a longer one. Of course she is at liberty to charge what she likes, but most home visits are to elderly pensioners. She imagines Betty Cohn in her stained cardigan, or bony Celia Duffy with her colostomy bag, fumbling in their purses for a tightly folded hundred-dollar bill while she waits with palm outstretched. Grubby, very grubby. That is surely not what medicine is about. But increasingly it is. Whether or not to charge for one's services is really no longer a philosophical or political question, rather it has become a question of survival. In the context of practising good medicine, universal bulk-billing is unsustainable. She knows this to be true. She has done the mental arithmetic repeatedly. But it is tiring and annoying and still somewhat demeaning that she has to factor money into her work.

Can she honestly say that money has never been a driving force in her life, despite the community stereotype, the fallback position of politicians: that doctors are greedy and self-serving? She wants to be able to say it. Her parents, both teachers in government schools, were motivated by intellectual rigour and a desire to do good. She believes she has absorbed these values so completely that the thought of being affluent seems almost immoral. She can see, now, how her parents' values were so clearly reflected in her career choice, although at the time of choosing, at the age of seventeen, she would have resisted the notion of parental influence. But she was not, at that unformed age, resistant to the notion of doing good. *I want to work with people, to help people*, she would say, when asked about her reasons for selecting medicine. She was not alone in this: many of her peers, especially the young women, gave this as their reason, too. And what else could they say? *I chose it for the prestige, for the comfortable living it will afford me.* When they had opted for a caring profession, how could they give expression to such calculating ambition, even if it were true? When she asks herself now, as she often does, why she chose the way she did, the answer comes back as a question: *What did you know, an unformed seventeen-year-old, about choice?* But still she clings to the notion that, at a time in her youth, a time that can be reduced again and again, from a nebulous swirl of influences and experiences that began *in utero*, reduced down to one decisive moment, perhaps the moment she entered the number '1'—a single, vertical stroke of the pen—against the word 'medicine' on the university application form: at that moment of choosing, she chose to do good.

But what use is it, this talk of good? She no longer knows the meaning of the word. It is an outdated word, stripped of its status as an abstract noun, now relegated to an insipid adjective, fast becoming an insipid adverb. Better to say she wanted *to help*; less lofty, more practical *to help* than to *do good*. In the scheme of things, she wants to be able to say that she chose to help. In preference to what? To standing by and doing nothing? To hindering? Being helped? Are these the choices she turned her back on? Would it have been better to choose neutrality or passivity? After what has happened, she can now say: yes, it would have been better to have chosen otherwise. Better for her and her patients. But increasingly she feels she must hold onto the notion of her seventeen-year-old self choosing to do good, even though she knows this to be a sentimental fancy, even though she knows the concepts of choice and goodness contained within her notion will not hold up to scrutiny of any kind, that she is incapable of defending them. Yet, if she does not cling to this one idea—this imperfect, hollow plank, torn from the sinking vessel—what, then, is there left to cling to?

In the evenings, when Paul is watching *The 7.30 Report* or *Four Corners*, she looks at him and wonders what it is that keeps them together. He must sometimes think the same about her. It is not that she feels they no longer have anything in common, or that they have drifted apart because of lack of interest. She would like to think they were less predictable than that. Her reflections are based more in the general than the specific. It is the nature of long-term relationships in general that she questions.

She usually brings a basket of washing into the room to fold while she watches television. She sits on the sofa with the basket at her feet and puts the washing on the floor in piles, one for each family member. She does not ask him to help her, but often, without a word, he will start taking clothes from the basket and folding them, his eyes still on the television screen. He takes a particular interest in matching the socks. Sometimes, when she looks at the folded socks piled between them on the sofa, the odd ones draped over the side of the basket (he matches them but does not know whose they are, apart from his own), she is struck by how far they have come.

When she met him all those years ago, at a student party, she had first thought him an artist. It might have been his long hair, falling over his eyes, or the angle at which he leaned against the wall in that Carlton terrace, as if he were aware of the line of his body, the figure he cut in the narrow hallway. Such self-awareness she might have construed as conceit in other men, but not in him. He was a final-year architecture student, he told her: an artist of sorts. She had worn her party dress that night—a vintage dress of red roses, with a square-cut neck and a fitted waist. Perhaps it had made her seem braver than she felt.

They were so young! Where did it go, their youth? Forfeited, nibbled away in daily, hourly increments. And with it, their hard-edged idealism, softened and yielded to the capacity for compromise. Their youth is gone, but, in its place, they have gained the skill of compromise. It is hardly a fair trade. They have also learned to read each other's minds. She had once believed this to be a good thing, a sign of their like-mindedness. She would have even gone so far as to say they were made for each other. But if recent experience has taught her anything, it is that she can no longer simply accept things as given; that the paradigm can shift as quickly, as treacherously as desert sand, so that north becomes south, good becomes harm. Like the gradually coinciding menstrual cycles of women who live together, their telepathy might be explained away by geography and routine: shared roof, shared mortgage, shared childcare, shared chores. She, despite her scientific view of the world, was once moved enough to believe in destiny and affinity. Now, in a world that makes less and less sense, she scrabbles in the dirt for rational explanations.

April 16

She visits a periodontist at his sleek rooms in the city. He deftly probes each of her teeth, calling out a number every time to his nurse, who writes them down on a card. 'You have moderately severe periodontitis,' he tells her when he has finished. 'You'll need gum surgery to slow the advancement of the disease. Even so, with the very best care, you're likely — almost certain — to lose one or two teeth.'

She hears his words and understands he is going through his patter — X-rays, review appointments, payment plans — but she can take none of it in. 'How long have I had this problem?'

'It's difficult to say. Most people have chronic disease over years, but some — a few — have a more rapidly advancing form. At this stage I can't say definitively which category you fall into.'

'But it's likely to have been present for a couple of years, at least?' Is she putting words into his mouth? If so, let him be the one to reject them.

The periodontist glances swiftly at his watch; she is detaining him with her questions but she does not care.

'A couple of years—yes, most likely.'

'And my dentist should have informed me of it? And commenced treatment?'

'Yes, if he or she had detected it. We've known how to diagnose and treat periodontitis for twenty years now—dentists included.'

Brian Leonard had been of the old school: superficially charming, urbane. He called her 'gorgeous' and tickled her under the chin as she sat in the chair, continuing this practice unabashed until she was well into her teens. He was an out-and-out flirt, a soft-skinned ladies' man, manicured and scented, his dark, wavy hair becoming ever more streaked with silver over the years. She remembers how her mother, his contemporary, would laugh and blush at his comments, delivered with a suggestive smile, a flash of his square white teeth (all capped, she now thinks: those teeth were too white, too regular). As a child she was fascinated by the large signet ring, studded with a red stone, on his little finger and the heavy gold chain bracelet that slid up and down his bare forearm as he worked. No other men she knew wore jewellery. He must have been only thirty when she first visited him, yet how experienced he seemed to her then; experienced and self-assured. He never explained, never educated. *Leave it to me*, his manner implied. *I am the professional here.* He did not encourage prevention: he did not even show her how to floss. Why, then, did she put up with it—his patronising manner, his sexist remarks—for so many years, when all such traits had become unacceptable in *her* profession? Because he was of the old school and she forgave him for it. She tolerated his behaviour because he and his fusty waiting room with its tattered children's annuals and humming fish tank were, for better or worse, a part of her childhood. She had first encountered him when she was willing to believe in the infallibility of adults. Her mother had delivered her to him. For these reasons she continued to *let him get away with it*.

But no longer. She telephones the office of the Health Services Commissioner and lodges her complaint. That night, when the boys are in bed, she goes to the computer and downloads the complaint form. There are numerous requests for information: dates of treatment, reports from other treating practitioners, an inventory of expenses. The whole document is compiled of facts and figures, but how will facts and figures convey how she feels? In frustration she takes a piece of paper and begins to write: *I have just been told that I have periodontitis—moderately severe, the periodontist informs me. Do you know what this means? I ask this because it seems you have failed to detect it, despite the many visits I have made to you over the years. My new dentist picked it up straight away.*

She knows this is unfair—the disease will have progressed over the last eighteen months—but the balance of fairness is still in her favour. Didn't she always pay her dental bills on time? Didn't she bring her boys to see him, driving forty minutes across town, trusting her children's teeth to his care? And he didn't even notice Joe's tongue-tie. She feels a fresh surge of anger.

Her cheeks burn. *You also failed to detect my son's tongue-tie. Neither did you inform me of his defective tooth enamel. Aren't these exactly the sort of conditions a dentist is supposed to discuss with his patients? What was I paying you for?*

She puts aside her letter and goes to the bathroom to again examine her mouth. She is making a habit of it, she knows that. She is increasingly compelled to look in the mirror, to lift her upper lip away from her top teeth and stare at her ravaged gums. She examines each tooth in turn, comparing one to the next, hoping—irrationally, she knows—that somehow her condition will have magically improved since the last time she looked. There remains, somewhere locked down deep, a feeling that it is simply not true, that she will wake up and realise this disfigurement she now suffers is but a drawn-out dream, that when she looks again in the mirror her gums will be perfectly formed, her smile will be dazzling.

'Focusing on the problem only makes things worse.' Paul is standing in the bathroom doorway, arms folded. 'You have to take your mind off it.'

She turns away from the mirror. 'That's easy for you to say. Half *your* teeth aren't about to fall out.'

'You know it isn't as bad as that. You'll have treatment and things will settle down.'

'No, you're wrong. The damage is already done. Things won't just settle down: they will continue to get worse. It's too late for platitudes.' She brushes past him and goes back to the study, back to her letter.

The worst of it is that this problem could have been prevented, she writes. *Why didn't you advise me on my brushing technique? Why didn't you tell me to floss? I would have taken your advice.* If only, years ago, he had told her to floss. She would still have healthy gums; shining pink gums, almost translucent, with scalloped edges that taper to a fine point between the teeth. Having started to notice other people's teeth, she knows how beautiful healthy gums can be. *Instead I now have a disease that, in addition to costing thousands of dollars in treatment, has left me disfigured.* Can she say that? Someone who loses a leg is disfigured: everyone would agree on that. Does she have the right to lay claim to such a word? But why should she care? An extravagant word strewn here and there is nothing to what he has done. *Disfigured* is nothing. She should call him a charlatan, incompetent, a creep! *I had always assumed, in this day and age, that people of my generation would keep their teeth.* Isn't that why she visited him, put up with his silly banter—his sexist banter, verging on sexual harassment—and paid all his bills? *Now I am told that I am likely to lose mine.* How will it happen? Gradually at first: a gap here and there. But then, all at once, the forces exerted by chewing will become too much for the remaining teeth, already compromised, and the whole system will collapse. Teeth will fall like skittles. Should she start now on puréed food, to at least delay the inevitable? *I am only forty-three. This should not be happening to someone my age. This should not be happening to me.*

After work the next day she again looks through the complaint form. She is required to provide dates of dental treatment over the past five years. With a thumping heart she dials the number of her former dental clinic, still in her address book. She gives her name. 'I am an old patient of Doctor Leonard's. I would like to get some information, please: a list of appointment dates.'

She has not thought of a false reason for her request but the receptionist does not ask for one. 'I'll just find your card,' she says brightly. She waits, the phone to her ear. She hears a filing cabinet being opened and then, transmitted down the line, across the city, as if through time, the sharp buzz of the doorbell, just as she remembers it. Once more she is there, at the receptionist's desk, the front door closing on the sunlight behind her, the flock-papered waiting room on her right. She hangs up the phone before the receptionist returns. The paperwork, close to completion, lies on the desk in front of her. She picks it up and tears it into pieces.

'How are you going with the complaint about your dentist?' Paul asks her that evening before bed.

She is sitting on the bed, applying hand cream. 'I have decided not to go ahead with it,' she says.

'Why not?' He checks himself and adds quickly: 'Not that I wanted you to proceed; in fact I think it's much better for you that you don't. But you seemed so determined. Why have you changed your mind?'

She closes the jar of cream. 'Because I have forgiven

him.' She holds her arms out wide. 'Brian Leonard, you are forgiven. Go in peace.' With her right hand she makes the sign of the cross in the air.

Paul frowns. 'You don't mean it, then.'

'Do I mean that I have forgiven him? That isn't the point. If he were still in practice I would proceed, so that other patients could be protected, at least. But he's an old man; retired now and out of harm's way. What good will complaining do me, or anyone else?'

'So you think you can put this behind you?'

'I have plenty of other matters to occupy my thoughts. But if you're asking if I forgive him, then, no, I don't.'

April 21

Sometimes, after a particularly demanding day, her imagination runs wild. The patients leave the clinic and, in her mind, they do not heed her advice. Today she saw a young woman whose serology for hepatitis B shows her to be a carrier of the disease. She spent the consultation explaining the nature of carrier status: how the virus can be transmitted to others through sexual contact and blood. 'Your boyfriend must be tested immediately, and be vaccinated against hepatitis B if he has no immunity. This is extremely important.' She must have said this three times, at least. But on the way home from work, idling at the traffic lights, she imagines the young woman leaving the clinic and throwing the brochure on hepatitis B into a bin at the street corner. She sees the young woman going home that evening and, hugging her secret to herself, having sex with her boyfriend as if nothing had changed. She tries to tell herself that what she has done for the young woman is good. She has diagnosed her patient's carrier status, thus enabling her to start monitoring her disease. Now the young woman can take the necessary precautions to avoid infecting others. She should be pleased. But instead she sees her young patient lying in her boyfriend's arms, sees the virus entering his unsuspecting body to take up residence there, and feels as if a direct path can be traced from him to her. It is as if by unearthing the virus she has become responsible for its behaviour, as well as the behaviour of those who harbour it. Waiting at the traffic lights, she knows already how this will end. She will phone her patient tomorrow and quiz her; ask that the boyfriend come in for a consultation so that she can witness, with her own eyes, his blood being taken for testing. A few days later she will hold, in her own hand, the pathology report of his hepatitis B status. She will ask, if he is not yet infected, that he come to see her for vaccination, so that she herself can inject the vaccine, can observe the needle pierce his skin and the contents of the syringe empty. Three times she will inject him, then, to make quite sure, she will retest his immunity. Only then will her responsibility end. All this will bring her no sense of achievement; instead, just a short-lived relief. She trusts only herself, her own eyes and hands, to do the job, to see it through. Who else can she rely on? Who else would go as far to protect her?

A new patient, a young man, comes to request help for a drug problem. He has been smoking heroin for four months and wants to stop. As she might have predicted, he has made a fifteen-minute appointment and she is already running behind. She probes for psychosocial problems as the root cause of his drug use: the end of a relationship, a history of depression, a dysfunctional family life. No, he tells her, everything is fine. A new group of friends, a new pastime, that is all. He has tried other drugs before. Maybe he will try something else in the future: he cannot be sure how things will go. Right now he is tired of the after-effects: the lethargy, the moodiness. He has tried to stop cold turkey a couple of times but he vomits and the muscle cramps are too painful. Can she give him something to help him withdraw?

The situation is not ideal but, then, it hardly ever is. She cannot afford to defer treatment. Who knows what he might do next? She examines him quickly then writes a prescription, as well as a list of over-the-counter medications. She writes down individual symptoms on the list and matches them to the appropriate medication with an arrow: for each ache or spasm, a pharmaceutical remedy. Let him now sit propped up in bed, like a crotchety old man with influenza, dipping every hour into the pill box on the bedside table. For the twisting of his bowels, a blue capsule; for the throbbing in his skull, a pink tablet. For the smoky voices of his dreams that call him back to the opium den, she has no pill to offer.

'Please come back in two days,' she says. 'I want to see how you are getting on.' She knows by the look in his eyes—half closed against the light coming in through the window behind her: should she have closed the blinds a little for him?—he will not make a follow-up appointment. It is not that the consultation has not delivered what he requested. He has left with a prescription. Isn't that what all drug users want? He has been given the opportunity to talk about his problems. It is more that he knows she is going through the motions, doing what is required rather than what is needed. He senses, quite rightly, that she does not care.

How can she defend her position, to him or anyone? She would like to think it is not that she does not care about *him*: a young man, barely out of adolescence; quite possibly, when not under the influence, a loving son, a good companion. But she finds it hard to concern herself with the details of his drug use—what he uses, when and why. Neither does she really care whether he uses again. His decision to use or abstain will depend on his biochemical make-up, his level of self-preservation, the influence of his peers: factors beyond her control, out of her reach. In both the problem and the solution she cannot, in this instance at least, be implicated.

She has wondered before why it is she is not tempted—has never really been tempted—by drugs of any kind, despite the occasional cautious experimentation of her university days. Given her current situation, why is she not tempted to escape, even just for a few hours, into her own velvet-curtained opium den? A silently descending curtain of the thickest, plushest velvet: she imagines that is what heroin is like, although she has never thought to ask. True, she has taken the odd sleeping pill from the sample packets in her surgery, has swallowed them, in secret, on those nights when sleep will not come, but, apart from this, her abstinence has been exemplary.

Why this resistance, if that is what it is?

Not for legal or medical reasons particularly; certainly not because she feels she must practise what she preaches. Perhaps it is because she has observed that drugs and alcohol are a short-term refuge; that, all too soon, the crutch becomes the problem. She has often read in the quarterly Medical Board bulletins of the shameful deeds of drug-addicted doctors: the falsifying of records, the writing of prescriptions for opiates in other people's names. She cannot descend into such behaviour; she feels shamed enough already. She thinks of the young man she has just seen: how he regarded her across the desk, squinting against the glare. Did he watch her as she wrote the prescription; observe, through half-closed eyes, the set of her jaw, the line of her mouth and see disapproval, even hard-heartedness written there? *Love the sinner, hate the sin.* She wants to care. But what could he be thinking, this young man, each time he uses? Does he not stop to consider consequences, the payment that will be irrevocably exacted, in one form or another? Heroin, the drug of the would-be hero: the promise of a fleeting communion with the gods. Then, when back on earth, a visit to the doctor (a fifteen-minute appointment!) to pick up the pieces, to stave off the pangs of longing. Why should she care, when she, despite her situation, resists all temptations? She, too, could be weak but she chooses to resist. She has given him his fifteen minutes. She has given him his script. What right does he have to ask more of her?

Rohan pokes his head around the door of the treatment room, where she is cleaning up after a procedure. 'Hey, I've only just realised something. I saw that boy's mother, just a few weeks ago.'

She knows immediately which boy. She motions him inside and asks him to close the door. 'What do you mean, you saw her?'

'As a patient. She was using a different surname. Pleasance, she called herself: probably her maiden name. But the boy's name is something else, isn't it?'

'Feltham.'

'Yes, so I didn't put two and two together until Margaret told me. She's only just worked it out, too. She didn't recognise her when she came in under her new name. Apparently she's changed a bit.'

She steadies herself. 'You mean she looks different?' She shouldn't ask. She knows Rohan's answer will set her off. He has never been one to mince words.

'Not just that. She seemed a bit loopy. Asking about vague symptoms, shooting pains in her head, tingling, that sort of thing—wanted a full check-up, then got angry when I tried to pin her down. Pretty much stormed out.' He shrugs. 'I won't see her again. Margaret will tell her it's not appropriate.'

Later she goes back through the appointment diary. Yes, there is the name, *Virginia Pleasance*, listed for the first of April. April Fools' Day. The same day she had gone to her car after work to find a deep scratch in the paintwork, running from boot to bonnet along the driver's side.

She has a visit to make on her way home, a quick one, she hopes. She mistakenly turns left one street before she should and at the end of the street she comes to a dead end. To reach her patient's house she can either get back in the car or cut through the small park that borders the two streets. It will be quicker to go on foot.

Save for the possums that move in the overhead branches, the park is empty. It is also unlit. In her doctor's bag she carries pethidine and diazepam, needles and syringes. An addict would have a field day, were they to step out from behind a tree this very minute and bail her up. She doesn't even have a phone with her. She quickens her pace. As she leaves the park and crosses the road she thinks of that outreach clinic where, years ago, she worked at night. On the slower evenings in winter, when the cold kept people away, she would sit and talk with Glenda, the practice receptionist. Glenda wore a built-up shoe, and eye make-up of theatrical proportions: aqua eye shadow that reached to her eyebrows, eyeliner to rival Cleopatra's. Her lashes, top and bottom, were clogged with the blackest mascara. Just the two of them at night in that godforsaken place, where anyone could walk in off the street and make demands of any kind. She must have been mad to put up with such conditions. Yet nothing dangerous ever happened. One summer's evening a gang of boys had climbed onto the tin roof: the thumping of feet and the swearing had carried down into the consultation room. Hardly a risky situation. Besides, Glenda had quickly sorted it out. 'I'll tell all your mums if you don't bugger off this minute,' she had shouted from the pavement outside. Glenda was a local, born and bred. In the waiting room the old men would grumble to her about the price of bread and cigarettes, the decline of the neighbourhood. Glenda would nod her head to their complaints then put a finger to her lips as she answered the phone. Even the hard-bitten adolescents, sent in by their youth workers, treated her with a sullen respect. With a lift of her pencilled eyebrows, she could send the drug reps scurrying. Was Glenda the only reason she had ever stayed safe? *Glenda*, she thinks as she knocks on her patient's front door, *where are you now?*

April 25

She takes a train to the city to meet with her solicitor, John, and Brendan Conroy, a medical advisor with her defence association. Book in hand, she attempts to read but finds her attention wandering from the page to the other passengers. There are many young people on the train, probably students on their way to university, casually dressed in jeans and T-shirts, their backpacks slung over one shoulder or sitting between their feet. Across the aisle sits a young man and opposite him, two young women. All three are involved in a conversation about mutual friends, it seems. The young man is good-looking—nice eyes, an engaging, intelligent manner. He sits forward in his seat, smiles and listens. He is a good listener: an attractive trait in a man. The girl in the seat closest to hers wears a baseball cap through which her long, blonde ponytail is threaded. When she smiles she shows small, even teeth; the kind of teeth that only years of orthodontics can produce. From her seat she cannot properly see the second girl, hidden behind the first: only her jean-clad legs and an occasionally extended arm, slight and heavily braceleted, are visible. The young man's eyes move from one girl to the other as each in turn takes up the conversation. Which girl does he care for? she finds herself wondering, for she believes he must care for one of them. He might not be entirely sure himself yet. Is he, even now, weighing the merits of one against the other, turning his attention to the blonde girl as she speaks, watching her mouth with its small, straight teeth and imagining the curve of her naked breasts as he nods his head in agreement with her opinions, then turning to the other with similar intent? If she could see the other girl she could form her own opinion of his preference, but she would have to leave her seat or otherwise lean conspicuously forward to see the obscured girl's face. By their flirtatious tone and the frequency with which his comments are sought, she senses the young women are competing for his attention. She is suddenly envious of this young man, desired by two women, possibly by others, too: perhaps there is a flock, a bevy of young women whose hearts beat harder in his presence. As if sensing her thoughts, the young man glances across the aisle towards her and for an instant their eyes meet. Embarrassed, she turns away and looks out the window.

As the train pulls into Prahran station the trio collect their bags and stand up to leave. The second young woman files out of her seat behind her friends: she is small, waif-like with cropped dark hair streaked with purple and a nose-stud in the shape of a flower. Her bracelets jangle as she slings her bag onto her shoulder. From her appearance, a different type from the other two—more artistic, more at the margins. And yet, there she is, at the door of the carriage, gazing up at the young man with a winning smile. But not winning enough. The carriage doors open and the small girl leaves first. Behind her, the blonde girl slips her hand into the young man's and, briefly but unambiguously, he squeezes it. As the train draws away she has her last glimpse of the trio, now walking shoulder to shoulder, the young man in the middle, his hands tucked into his pockets. She sees the waif-girl open her mouth to laugh, having not yet realised—perhaps she will know soon, perhaps later that day—she has been passed over for another; she has not been chosen.

In the past, in her youth and all that followed, did she take success for granted? When she got the entry marks for medicine—standing at the letterbox on that January morning, squinting against the sun already fierce in the sky, the transcript of results open in her trembling hands—did she spare a thought for the others whose marks would not allow them to hope? For those who had wanted to do medicine more than she; for those who, given the chance, might have been better doctors than she has turned out to be? In the days that followed her letter of acceptance into medical school, did she ever question her elation or try to divine its source? She would be a doctor, she had achieved her goal: was that all it was? Or was there a darker agenda? She would be a doctor *because she had done better than most*. She had succeeded where others had failed. Could it be that success, in her terms at least, has come at the expense of others? What are her life's achievements? Her medical-school graduation, ranked eighteenth in the year; her general-practice fellowship; the birth of her children: these are the things that immediately come to mind. She begins to remember the smaller things, too: a poem, written when she was thirteen, published in the school magazine; a patient whose colon cancer she discovered, after the specialist had missed it. What does this litany tell her? She can see a pattern emerging; a pattern of endeavour and competition, a ranking of herself against others. But the birth of her sons? How can she see that in a competitive light? Childbirth is an achievement, everyone knows that, but is the joy it engenders derived, even in part, from the failure of others? Her two boys, each a little overdue, were born pink-skinned and vigorous, each pronounced at her bedside by Paul—as he kissed their sticky foreheads—to be perfect. Can she honestly say she would have been as joyous if they were not?

She sits with John and Brendan at the table in the conference room, the files spread out before them. She has the beginnings of a headache, an insistent throbbing in her left temple, and, in the pit of her stomach, a feeling of impending negativity. She must be premenstrual.

'I notice, now, the bad press doctors get, especially on talkback radio.' She pushes her chair away from the table. 'Was it always like this?'

Brendan looks up from his reading. 'Doctors are an easy target. The community sees us as powerful and privileged. With privilege comes accountability: at least that's how it's been since the eighties, when the concept of accountability became enshrined in the public consciousness.' He smiles encouragingly. 'But doctors get good press, too: medical breakthroughs, marathon operations, that sort of thing.'

She ignores this last remark. 'People seem to take great pleasure in going on talkback radio and divulging the details of their medical conditions, so that they can then tell stories of the incompetence or heartlessness of doctors they have had dealings with. You might find this too defensive—or perhaps, in view of what has happened, rather recalcitrant of me—but I can't help thinking people have got it wrong. They blame the individual rather than the profession. Somehow the profession has evolved to a situation where mistakes are intolerable.' *The legal profession has assisted in this*, she wants to say. *The legal profession has led people to believe that doctors should be infallible and fallibility should be punished.* She takes a deep breath. She must stop seeing lawyers as the enemy. John is not her enemy. 'Any person doing what we do would sometimes make mistakes or, at the very least, be abrupt or dismissive every now and then. Those who haven't done it can't understand what it is like to see a new patient every fifteen minutes, to be required to listen carefully to everything they say, to examine them and provide a solution, a diagnosis, a plan of management in a considerate and courteous way, then turn around and immediately do it again in the next quarter of an hour.'

There is silence. John looks at his watch. Has she

overstepped the mark? Perhaps John has understood the subtext of her speech. Well, so what? There he sits, shuffling paper, no doubt paid handsomely by the hour, while she is paid nothing, less than nothing. He can afford to hear some home truths. All these documents, these reams of paper: all words and no meaning! She would like to sweep them all onto the floor. Or throw them in his face.

'How many medical-negligence cases have you worked on now?' she asks him abruptly, massaging her temples.

John looks wary. 'It must be close to thirty.'

'And what is your opinion of my case? Where do I stand?'

'Where do you stand, with respect to the law?'

'With respect to the law—yes, I suppose so.'

'As far as the law goes, you have a case to answer.'

'Then the law is a waste of time. I knew that three years ago.'

John and Brendan exchange a glance. 'This isn't easy for you, Anna. I understand that,' Brendan says evenly. 'But we must go on. You've been served a writ and you have only two choices: to defend the claim or settle. You do not have the choice of opting out.' His voice takes on an edge. 'John and I are working in your best interests and I would encourage you to think of your situation in that way. When you feel frustrated, try asking yourself: "At this point, what course of action is in my best interests?"'

'Before this happened, I never thought about my interests. I always tried to act in the best interests of my patients. That was my job—to consider the good of my patients at all times. Now you are saying I must put my interests over those of a patient.'

'Yes, you must, because, in this case, your interests and those of the plaintiff are in conflict,' John says. 'Besides, he is no longer your patient. He brought the charges. You have the right to defend yourself.'

'Yes, I understand.' Her head is throbbing badly. 'I just wish we could have settled straight away, instead of dragging it out like this.'

'You know what the plaintiff was asking for initially,' Brendan says. 'If we settled every case without mounting a defence, the insurance premiums would be so prohibitive that doctors would go elsewhere. We simply can't operate like that.'

'And yet, if it had been a clear-cut case of negligence, you would have had no choice but to settle. Instead, I am forced to go on answering question after question. This repeated dissection of a single page of notes and a few conversations with a patient that together lasted less than an hour ... I'm sorry but I simply cannot respect a system that allows a doctor to be punished for a lesser, rather than a greater, degree of negligence.'

John has begun to pack up his briefcase. 'You may not be able to respect the process but I'm afraid you must accede to it. The law applies to doctors, too.'

John has left the meeting, his feathers ruffled, no doubt, by her outburst. She stays at the table, hunting through her bag for some paracetamol while Brendan fetches her a glass of water.

'Anna, would you like to reconsider the offer of counselling?' he asks on his return. He sits down beside her. 'I know you felt it unnecessary when we first discussed it, but things change. Doctors often find their stress increases as we move closer to trial.'

For most of his working week, Brendan is an anaesthetist. As a speciality, anaesthetists are not known for their interpersonal skills. She cannot fathom why he works here. 'To tell you the truth, even if I wanted counselling, I just don't have the time to fit it in.'

It seems Brendan is not to be deterred. 'Try not to blame yourself too much,' he goes on. 'Osteosarcoma is notoriously difficult to detect in its early stages. It's a mistake many of your peers would have made. The fact that we are prepared to run your case, to take it to court if needs be, means that we believe that we—you—have a good chance of winning.'

'It doesn't seem right to talk of winning, when a boy has lost his leg.'

'Given this adversarial legal system, winning and losing are apt terms. Of course having cancer and needing an amputation are difficult, undesirable things for a young man: no one is trying to deny that. But the question is: to what extent are you, Doctor Anna McBride, legally responsible? That is what is under examination here. Your morality is not on trial. You must keep telling yourself that.'

The page on which she wrote her notes about Ben Feltham—four entries in all—has become an historical document. A single page of shorthand prose, uninspired and somewhat lacking, yet what countless pages have been generated from its study! Pages enough to swell files and fatten briefcases, to cover the conference table in a rustling quilt of black and white. The questions the other side has concocted! As if every word of her clinical notes—written in a hurry, between patients, her hand untidy—held multiple meanings, sinister meanings. They have even questioned the colour of the ink in which she wrote her first entry. 'Weren't two different blue pens used?' they asked. They would have the ink analysed.

'A blue pen is a blue pen,' she had said to John. 'How can they make anything of it?'

'They are trying to imply that you have altered your notes at some later stage,' John had said. 'You must provide an explanation for the use of different pens, or they will use it against you.'

That she is interrogated about such things! *I am not a criminal*, she wants to say to John. *There was no intent to harm. Doesn't that count for something?*

A single page, on which her fate is written. If she could but tear up that page, and throw it into the fire. She would watch its corners curl, see the flames lick at her diagram of his knee, crudely drawn, the site of his pain shaded with diagonal lines. What exquisite relief to see those three letters—*PFS*—scorched beyond recognition! PFS: patellofemoral syndrome. (*Wrong!*

Wrong! She did not think to ask about night-time pain.)
If she could burn that page, erase it from history and
start again. If she could but start again.

April 28

A mother brings in her toddler with a nondescript rash. 'She played with another child five days ago,' the girl's mother says, 'and that child now has chickenpox. Is that what my daughter has, too?'

The child is well and her rash is not that of varicella. Besides, the incubation period is far too short. Has the girl been immunised? Yes, she has. Then there is nothing else to do but wait a while longer. If the child does get chickenpox, which is very unlikely, the infection will most probably be mild.

She explains this to the girl's mother as best she can: still, she senses the woman's scepticism. The other child has a rash, now her child has a rash, the woman is thinking. Surely these events are connected. Would that it were always so simple. She could coax this woman into divulging her doubts. She could be warm and understanding, employ a bit of humour. But her neck hurts, she is running behind and she does not feel like laughing.

Where is the beginning and end of an illness? Before Ben Feltham happened by, she would never have thought to ask. Now it seems like a pertinent question: she might suggest the lawyers use it in her defence. Is this the sort of information John wants her to provide? Is this what he means by the team approach?

The time period of some acute diseases—a common cold, a case of chickenpox—can be measured, more or less. Contacts can be traced and exposure thereby pinpointed. Incubation periods for most common infections are already known. The onset of the disease phase announces itself with definite symptoms: fever, a rash, a sore throat. Then the symptoms subside and the disease is said to have ended.

The course of more chronic diseases, their beginnings and ends, cannot be so readily measured. She is warming up to this line of argument: surely, here lies her chance. Cancer, for example, occurs at a cellular level—unregulated mitosis, the doubling and redoubling of renegade cells—a long time, sometimes years, before it is clinically manifest, as a lump in the breast, a swelling of the bone. Remove the breast, amputate the bone and carve out the lump. Slice through it, stain it and see under the microscope the disarray, the ugliness.

But what of the *end* of an illness? What of the end of a cancer? Can it be said the disease is ended once the tumour is cut away and the breast reconstructed, the stump fashioned? Her argument has crumbled into dust. People speak of cancer changing their lives. Will Ben Feltham speak of it this way when he is twenty-five? When he is sixty? Will he be around at sixty to speak of anything?

Think! Think! There must be another way out. Susceptibility to certain diseases is programmed into one's DNA: in effect these diseases start at conception. Should a patient therefore blame a doctor for failing to detect the earliest manifestations of their illness? Now she is on to something. Should they instead be accusing their own parents or grandparents of passing on their genetic predisposition to such an illness? Could she, too, blame her parents for passing on, through their DNA or their example, or maybe both, some sort of insufficiency—organic or otherwise—that led her to make an inappropriate decision, the wrong decision, about a patient? Her father, dead for the past five years. He had been in the garden, cutting the lawn with the old push-mower. Silently, in the shade of the jacaranda, the grass half-mown. Her mother had found him that evening, his body showered with purple flowers. *Forgive me, Dad. How could I blame you for anything?*

Can she blame her medical training? Were her teachers negligent in their duty of care? Perhaps they should have taught her to practise more defensively, leaving nothing to chance or the passage of time. She thinks back again to that needle-stick injury on the gastrointestinal ward: the needle that jabbed deeply into her thumb. Did something happen then? Did some as yet unidentified organism, some rare blood-borne prion, enter her body, slowly and subtly infiltrating her consciousness so that, at one particular moment in her life, one crucial moment, her judgement was clouded, her insight impaired? In short, can she blame someone else for her troubles?

Where is the beginning and end of responsibility? She finds it hard now to draw the line. But, really, she need not concern herself. It is no longer her business, if it ever were. The line has been drawn for her by Ben Feltham's lawyers and she is on the wrong side of it. She is responsible. She is to blame.

The shifting sands of her marriage. Do other people live like this? She is not sure she can continue to put one foot so carefully in front of another, never knowing where the fault-line might be. Things might go steadily for a day: they manage to circumnavigate each other during breakfast, one showering while the other eats, one dressing the children while the other leaves, the one who remains behind hearing the front door close, the car backing down the driveway, the fading noise of the engine. These circles of avoidance widen every day: will the house soon be too small to hold them both? At least, on days such as these, there is an absence of words, a silence that allows her, if not respite from thinking, then respite from thoughts of a more violent, insistent kind. Such days are neutral. Then suddenly, perhaps the following day, a word is let drop or is hurled from one to the other, and she turns to see him standing there, looking back at her. Is it that she sees him, then, as he is, or is her vision at these times distorted? For this is the essential question: at which times does she see things as they really are? At bad times he is physically changed: his jowls hang more heavily, the lines on his forehead are more pronounced, his body is thicker, more unyielding in its stance. He becomes a wall, an impediment. She cannot get around him, she cannot see past him.

At other times, she might glance into the children's bedroom and see him sitting on Joe's bed, see his hand brush the hair away from Joe's forehead so that Joe looks younger, smiling and refreshed, and she might remember how her father used to do the same. Perhaps this brushing of hair from a child's forehead is a fatherly thing: at once practical, yet providing the opportunity to touch the child's face. At such times Paul seems slighter, his body more yielding, his skin smoother in the soft light of the bedside lamp. Can she love him then? But who does not warm to the image of the gentle father at the bedside, the paternal hand that sweeps the hair from the face and lingers on the cheek, the low voice that, underneath the words of the bedtime story, says to the enthralled listener: *I am strong and fierce in my love for you. I will protect you forever.*

What to think about, now, during sex? She feels she must sort this out, to prepare herself. What did she used to think about? She does not believe—can she not remember?—the sexual act was ever all-consuming: there was always a conscious viewing of herself in the bed, her conscious mind looking down, a little disapprovingly perhaps, upon her writhing body. She is not proud of this. She knows it to indicate a lack of physicality and spontaneity, qualities she envies in others. It could be her medical training that is at fault: having been taught to examine the body in an attempt to master it, she can no longer let the body master her. While she might never have been able to give herself up completely to the physical act, she has occasionally come close. There have been times, usually involving too much to drink, when she has almost switched off the cortical overseeing of sex (but can it be switched off at will?), come close to wallowing in brainstem sensations. But now, what to think about? Or rather, how to think? How to view the act when it is in progress? She is relieved they still have sex: this must be a good sign. She is grateful to Paul for this, although she understands Paul's motivation is not a charitable one. He has a physiological need; one he would probably rather not, under the circumstances, have to satisfy. So why is she relieved and grateful? Of course she knows it is not real gratitude she feels, but rather the veneer of it, sticky and brittle, a hasty attempt to conceal the defects beneath. This veneer, however shabby, must suffice for now.

The sensation of flesh upon flesh: in the consultation room this sometimes opens the floodgates. It has often been observed, both by herself and by others, that a patient who cannot or will not articulate the nature of his problem during the history-taking will find the words to open his heart during the examination, as she places her fingertips over his radial pulse, or palpates his abdomen with her open hand. She knows that legitimate physical contact between a doctor and patient, although restrained and clinical, can be, in a small way, therapeutic. And now, when Paul's skin touches hers, when his fingertips press into her flesh as he moves above her, she is aware of a similar desire to yield: to open the floodgates of her bursting heart. So she must prepare herself.

April 29

On her third visit to the periodontist he tells her she has a ten-millimetre pocket around a left upper molar. Has the tooth been sore, he asks? She remembers some pain on chewing a few months ago, which has since subsided. What does this ten-millimetre pocket mean? He suspects a root fracture, he tells her. He can see the tooth has already had root-canal surgery. She will need to have the tooth out, and soon. Leaving it there will only jeopardise the health of the surrounding teeth.

'How can you be sure it is fractured?' she asks. Specialist or not, expert or not, she will not let him remove her tooth on the basis of a hunch.

'If you're concerned about the diagnosis,' he says, 'I can first have a look by lifting the gum away from the root. If I find a fracture, as I'm certain I will, we can continue with the extraction.'

She is imposing upon him with her talk of making sure: at least, that is how he makes it sound. Well, it is *her* tooth, *her* mouth, *her* cheeks and lips that will sink inwards as her teeth are removed, one by one, and her jawbone shrinks away.

'Is there no alternative?' She is almost pleading. 'Can anything be done to save it?'

'Nothing whatsoever. Of course, we can always consider a dental implant afterwards.'

When she was twelve she had two teeth extracted: two upper premolars, one on each side. She remembers the pliers and cotton-wool swabs, and afterwards, having the rest of the day off school, during which she sat quietly and read a book her mother had bought her for the occasion. The gaps had been quickly filled by other teeth, jostling for position in her crowded mouth. At forty-three there will be no such recompense, no readjustment. The hole left behind, once the long molar roots are cleaved from the bone, will be permanent, like a scar. *One tooth, one child*: that is the old saying. If it is true, is she to lose two teeth, or three?

The medical term for miscarriage is abortion. A threatened abortion is a pregnancy in limbo: one lies down, with a cold cloth on one's forehead and a pad between one's legs, one watches and waits. One might also pray, if one were so inclined. A woman who fully miscarries is said to have had a spontaneous abortion: spontaneous here is used in the sense of 'natural' rather than 'voluntary' or 'unpremeditated'. *It is nature's way*, people often say, but it does not help. A missed abortion is a silent miscarriage, in which the foetus dies *in utero* and remains there for some time, perhaps weeks or even months, before its death is discovered by the doctor, who notices the uterus has stopped growing, or by the mother, who senses something is terribly wrong. The term 'missed abortion' is an odd one: missed by whom, one is moved to ask? The term and its ensuing question seem to imply a degree of negligence on the part of the woman, or her doctor.

Hers was spontaneous, at home in her bathroom, on the twenty-ninth of April, three years ago. She alone will commemorate it.

May 2

Joe is ill. She wakes in the night to his crying, and takes him to the bathroom to vomit. She wipes his mouth, gets him a drink of water and shepherds him back to bed. He is hot to the touch. The next morning he vomits again. His temperature is thirty-eight degrees and he complains of a headache. She considers asking her mother to look after him while she goes to work, as she has always done in the past. But instead she decides to phone the clinic and let them know she will not be in today. It is easier, these days, to make this decision, now that she has let go of all notions of indispensability.

When Joe wakes, later in the morning, he again complains of a headache. As he sits up in bed to swallow the analgesic liquid she offers, she observes that he is reluctant to flex his neck. She asks him to put his chin on his chest but he refuses, saying it is too sore to do so. His temperature is thirty-nine degrees. At the precise moment the thermometer beeps and she reads the number *39* in digital print, she feels the balance of probabilities relating to Joe's illness—a balance, until now, she has not consciously considered—suddenly shift. She has unconsciously attached to his condition the diagnosis of 'viral illness', non-specific and benign, the headache and vomiting secondary to the fever; symptoms of the fever rather than signs of any significance in themselves. Had she seen a child in the surgery with a similar presentation—headache, fever and vomiting—she would have been required to articulate this diagnosis to a parent; to explain her reasoning, to inform about treatment, prognosis and reasons for review. But when treating her own child, the process of diagnosis and management is inarticulate and piecemeal. Unlike a patient whom she observes at one point in time, her son she has intermittently, unsystematically observed over a period of hours, attending to his needs in an ad hoc fashion, distracted by the phone, the household chores. Her observation of the nature and progress of his illness, her clinical gaze, has been tainted with subjectivity; her observation of him has been diluted by time, distorted by the fact he is her son and the expectation, or hope, that he will not have a serious illness. So that now she sits on the edge of his bed, holding the thermometer in her hand, asking him again to try to bend his neck. The balance has shifted. She is now afraid he is seriously ill. The constellation of his symptoms and signs now signifies the possibility of something more sinister. His headache now takes on a darker significance in her mind; no longer simply the result of a fever, it now suggests, in combination with neck stiffness, underlying inflammation of the meninges. She is afraid he has bacterial meningitis.

She hurriedly pulls off his pyjama top and looks for a

rash, the purpuric rash of meningococcal disease. She is overreacting, she knows this instinctively, yet at the same time she chastises herself for complacency. She is aware of the dilemma of treating one's own family: the tendency to trivialise the illness on the one hand and, on the other, the tendency to panic, to interpret the symptoms in the most ominous light. But of which of these extremes can she now be accused? The objective evidence for meningitis stacks up: temperature, vomiting, neck stiffness. But her subjective filter, its opacity, its capacity for distortion: these things cannot be measured, at least not by her. The subjective clouds the objective, which, in turn, feeds into the subjective: the circular layering of fact upon perception. Between the subjective and objective she is caught, hamstrung.

She makes an appointment with the local GP. Even this is bad medicine, she thinks, as she dials the number: if she believes Joe may have meningitis, why then is she not rushing him to hospital? The doctor she normally sees is not in that morning, the receptionist tells her, so she makes the appointment with another doctor, whom she does not know. But Joe does not want to leave his bed to go to the doctor's surgery. As she coaxes him into his dressing-gown, she asks herself if it is for him she is doing this.

At the clinic they sit for twenty minutes in the waiting room, Joe's head against her shoulder, until the doctor, a woman of about her age, calls Joe's name. She does not tell the woman she, too, is a GP: not yet, anyway. Maybe she will surprise her at the end of the consultation. As much as possible she wants this doctor to keep to her routine, to think of her son as simply another patient, rather than the child of another doctor. The GP asks the questions and she answers briefly, holding herself back, resisting the desire to interpret, to prognosticate. Whenever possible, she lets her son answer: *it is his illness, not mine*, she tells herself. She does, however, tell the GP about the neck stiffness: this must be communicated. After all, that is the reason they are here. The GP nods attentively but does not look particularly anxious.

She has to admit, a little begrudgingly, that this GP is good to Joe. Through a trained eye she observes that the GP directs most of her comments to him, letting him know through her calm voice and genuine smile that she is concerned for him, that she wants to help. And, in the way she takes his hand in hers to lead him to the examination couch, she has already begun to help. Joe seems more relaxed, less fearful. Has he, then, been afraid all this time? Not just ill but afraid, too? From where has his fear come? Is it her fault he is afraid? In her distress, she has not attempted to hide her fear: she has been self-indulgent with it when it was her role as a doctor and a mother to allay fear. To take responsibility for fear: that is what her profession demands and motherhood requires. So she has failed. In diagnosis and management, in maternal care, she has failed dismally. Again she has failed.

The GP finishes examining Joe and turns to her. 'You are probably worried he has meningitis,' she says smoothly, 'but I don't believe that's what it is. Anyone who had meningitis with neck stiffness like Joe's wouldn't be sitting here, talking to me coherently, like he is doing. They would be extremely unwell, close to unconsciousness, whereas Joe is alert and well oriented. I think this is some sort of viral infection. I'm not entirely sure why he doesn't want to move his neck—perhaps his muscles are sore because of the infection. Anyhow, I don't think it's a serious problem. Take him home, give him paracetamol and put him to bed. Please call me later in the day to let me know how he is. Is there anything you would like to ask me?'

Yes, she has a question. *How is it that, in the polluted atmosphere of current medical practice—fear of litigation leading to defensive, bland medicine; the quiet-yet-seething hysteria that clouds every interaction with our patients—how is it you can make a clinical judgement and communicate it honestly to me, the mother of your patient and therefore your potential adversary? How is it that you can consider what is best for the patient, not what will provide you with the safest option? You leave yourself open, and yet you do it calmly, with certainty. How is it that you have escaped and I have not?* But she does not ask it. What would the poor woman think? *I would like to see you again*, she might say in a voice that was meant to be soothing. *Make a long appointment on your way out*. No, she will not ask her ridiculous question. Instead, she thanks the GP and takes Joe home to bed.

Her mother phones that evening to see how Joe is. Joe is improving, she tells her: his fever is down. She is about to hang up when her mother asks: 'Do you remember the time you picked up some dry cleaning on your bike and my dress caught in the wheel as you were riding home? You must have been about twelve.'

Has she been drinking? Her mother has never been one to tipple, never been known to make tremulous phone calls to her daughters after one too many brandies. But this nostalgia! From where does it flow, if not from the effects of alcohol? She senses a trap. 'Yes, I remember. The dress was torn.'

'Do you remember how upset you were?'

How dare her mother do this! 'You were upset, too,' she counters hotly. 'It was your best dress.' *Best dress!* What an antiquated term! She must extricate herself from whatever it is her mother has in mind. She is forty-three, no longer twelve: too old, too weary to play such games.

Her mother sighs. 'You so rarely made mistakes when you were young, Anna. You were always so careful, so painstaking. Maybe that is why this has hit you so hard.'

'What are you saying? That if I'd made more mistakes in my life, harming a patient wouldn't seem so bad? Making mistakes doesn't somehow confer immunity to the consequences of further mistakes. I'm sorry, but your logic is ridiculous.'

'Nobody blames you, Anna, darling. Nobody but yourself.'

Her eyes fill with tears: she is nobody's darling, not any more. She manages to keep her voice steady. 'Goodnight,' she says. 'Thank you for calling.'

It should be so simple. Love your children always. Waiting at the school gate, she sees them turn the corner, first Joe, skipping by himself, and then William, dawdling, talking with his friends. Her children stand out from the rest—their hair shinier, their expressions wiser, their smiles more endearing—and for a moment she is content. At that moment it feels enough. For a moment—for the time it takes her boys to walk around the corner of the school hall, along the path, to the front gate—it is enough. If she could understand the nature of unconditional love. If she could but measure and record its blend of sensory stimuli—the glint of the sun on her children's hair, the feel of her lips on their cheeks—its synaptic pathways and hormonal surges—serotonin for happiness, adrenaline for excitement, prolactin for the flow of maternal nurturance—measure, record and channel unconditional love, its tranquillising euphoria, at will. If she could love unconditionally and always, then nothing would matter: not the lost shoes, the scrapping and niggling, the muddy footprints in the hall, the whining, the obstinacy. She would conjure love to replace the pettiness of annoyance, the pangs of resentment. She would be the Madonna—blissful, serene, her overflowing bosom at the centre of the world. And if she could love Paul unconditionally. Could she do it? To love the bristling silences; the dirty dishes in the sink; the inconsistencies borne of lack of caring; the dirty bathroom basin; the lies—there have been lies, she is sure of it; the dirty, cowardly deceit: she would be happier, wouldn't she, if she could love all this, too?

Sometimes she forgets to kiss the boys before they leave for school. She cannot remember when last she kissed her husband.

May 5

A young woman comes to see her, complaining of one month of nausea, lethargy and feeling faint. 'I have become fussy about food,' she adds, 'and I have some indigestion.'

'Could you be pregnant?' It is her first question, her first thought.

'No. No, it's not possible.' The woman hesitates. 'At least, I don't think so.'

'How would it be, if you were?'

'No, I can't be.'

The young woman agrees to a pregnancy test and returns to the room with a sample of urine. Together they wait in silence: she, standing at the bench, her eyes on the test, the woman sitting anxiously in her seat.

After a minute a single line appears. 'It's negative,' she tells the young woman. She hands the test to her so she can see it with her own eyes. The woman exhales slowly and smiles: she is relieved. She does not want to be pregnant: not yet, anyway. There are many things she wants to do before having children. But now another cause of the woman's symptoms must be found.

She tries to rouse herself, to consider alternative diagnoses but she is unable to think clearly. Having been sure the young woman was pregnant, she now finds herself devoid of any other ideas. She sends her patient away with antacids and a request for a blood test, then sits slumped at her desk. What is wrong with her? What is it to her that the test was negative? Like her patient, she should also be relieved: the counselling of a woman with an unwanted pregnancy is not a task she enjoys. (She does it properly, she is kind, but she takes no pleasure in it.) So why this flatness, this sudden ennui, so early in the day?

Could it be that, at forty-three, she is becoming grandmotherly, looking for vicarious excitement in the pregnancies of fertile young women, waiting—like a wise, old crone—to pinch their cheeks with bony fingers and wink knowingly at their symptoms? She is certainly old enough to be a grandmother. A mother at twenty, a grandmother at forty: isn't that what nature intended? Strange to consider nature's intent, when most of her days are spent attempting to thwart this very thing. Each time she writes a script for antibiotics or immunises a child, doesn't she throw down the gauntlet to nature? One needs only to glance at the pharmacopoeia, as thick as her fist, to see how medical science has triumphed: for every trick of nature, a medical antidote. But a positive pregnancy test—that silent moment, that holding of breath, when the test becomes positive. (How many times has she seen those two pink lines emerge, first one and then the other, yet she never ceases to feel something: that tug at her heart.) *I have been taking the pill. How could I be pregnant?* the woman might ask, incredulous, although a part of her already understands. *These things can happen*, she might tell the woman. *Contraception sometimes fails.* And the pricking of her eyelids, the tug at her heart as she goes on with the consultation.

During her residency she worked on both the orthopaedic and vascular surgery wards, where amputations were almost commonplace. Motorbike or workplace accidents in which a limb was irreparably crushed or severed, the advancing gangrene of diabetic vascular disease: such were the usual reasons for amputation. What was done, then, with a limb, once it had been removed from the body? In the surgical wards the recovering amputees congregated in wheelchairs on the balcony to smoke, discussing operations and illnesses with the hard-nosed detachment of war veterans. They lifted their hospital-issue pyjamas to display their battle scars on abdomens, chests and legs, communally mourning their losses: the organs halved or removed completely, the limbs cut away. Some of them—those with diabetes and a smoking habit of forty or fifty a day—were bilateral amputees, sitting in the morning sun on the hospital balcony, resigned, so it seemed, to a myocardial infarct or cancer of the lung. Having lost both of their legs, they smoked for consolation. 'You have to stop smoking,' they were told by the consultants; the endocrinologists who managed their diabetes, the cardiologists who bemoaned the state of their coronary vessels, the vascular surgeons who would perform their next amputation. 'I can't,' or 'I don't want to,' they replied, grimly cheerful. But it had never been simply a question of willpower or choice. If only she had taken the time, away from her rostered duties, to sit on the balcony and listen to their stories. There might have been one or two of them, those recalcitrants, in whom—with the right word, the smallest encouragement, a nod of her head at a seminal moment—she could have triggered a change of heart. If she had tried, could she have saved a limb?

There was an incinerator at the hospital, down in the basement. She remembers the chimney, towering high above the wards, and the thin plume of dark, sweetish-smelling smoke that appeared at the end of the day. If she smelled that smoke again, she would know it immediately. Was there also a fine, grey ash that, on a windless evening, floated through the air as she left the hospital, her day's work done, and walked to her car? Can memory recapture the almost imperceptible feel of ash against the skin? But no matter, it is all in the past. The hospital of her residency is long gone, demolished for a luxury apartment block. And hospital incinerators, having been deemed an environmental hazard, are no longer in use.

Driving home from book club that evening, she turns on the car radio. The late-night program host is interviewing a woman—a 'holistic practitioner', he calls her—about children with attention deficit hyperactivity disorder.

'Does the medical profession properly understand this condition?' the interviewer asks.

'Absolutely not,' the woman replies.

It sounds as if she has been waiting for this question, waiting to pounce. The interviewee goes on to relate an anecdote about a child she knew who was diagnosed with ADHD on the basis of his answers to a questionnaire. 'This child could sit and play chess for hours,' she says. 'You cannot make a diagnosis of ADHD by questionnaire. You need a holistic approach to understanding this condition.' The discussion turns to medical treatment. 'I believe ADHD has a lot to do with diet,' the interviewee says, 'but the medical profession prefers to hand out dexamphetamines like lollies.'

She turns off the radio. She has a headache brewing: she should not have drunk red wine. The implication is, of course, that doctors would prefer to tally the score on a questionnaire or dash off prescriptions than take the time to consider their patients in the context of their individual circumstances. This accusation is often made, so there must be some truth to it, or at least the perception of truth. Doctors are still seen as slaves to science, to the acquisition of objective information: the general perception is that doctors value this type of information over the personal and the subjective. She could live with this perception, if that were simply the end of the matter, but it is not.

Despite what has happened, she has retained faith in the value of gathering objective information. A doctor cannot simply concur with what a patient says about their problem: what would be the sense in even seeing a doctor in that case? One might as well diagnose and treat oneself. A doctor must insert some systematic, methodical analysis into the interaction: that is, after all, what they are trained to do. Medical training is largely based in science, in the evidence collected from research undertaken according to scientific principles: this might not please some critics, but why blame individual doctors for the way they have been trained? But it is the subtext of this perception that wounds her.

She is so easily wounded these days: her skin has grown as thin as tissue paper. The woman on the radio has implied that doctors do these things—tally questionnaires, write prescriptions—not because they have been trained to believe in the value of these methods of diagnosis and treatment, but because they are corrupt in some way. They are cold and uncaring of their patients, they choose not to spend enough time with them, they enter into murky deals with pharmaceutical companies: these are the deeper, more sinister implications. But as a doctor she must ask, where is the evidence for this? *Show me the evidence that doctors do not care*. The holistic practitioner would probably scoff at her, but let *her* end up in court, defending a charge of negligence. When the prosecuting barrister ridicules *her*, again and again, for the lack of evidence for *her* management decisions, let *her* see, then, where her holistic approach has got her.

But she is making too much of this, upsetting herself about inconsequential remarks on an obscure late-night radio program. She has become far too sensitive to criticism, even of an impersonal kind. The fact of the matter is she should not have gone to book club. These meetings have become too much of a strain: the female laughter, in which she used to join unselfconsciously, now seems unnecessarily loud and strident. There is too much talk, when all she desires is silence. Why then does she still go? Why front up, month after month, bottle or plate in hand, to spend three difficult hours in the company of these women, her *friends*—but what does that mean now?—to come home exhausted and close to tears. Why do it? Paul encourages her to go because he thinks it does her good when, in reality, seeing other people laugh only heightens her awareness of her own bleak state of mind. Is this Paul's motivation? she wonders. Perhaps it is for his good, not hers, that she leaves the house. But she continues to go out of pride. *She soldiers on, cutting off her nose to spite her face*, simply for *the sake of appearances*: she is foolish and stubborn and *her own worst enemy*. She knows exactly what the other women would say about her if she were not there.

May 7

Bridget, a friend from book club, has asked to meet her for coffee. She was initially reluctant, but Bridget insisted. 'I need to talk to you,' Bridget said on the phone. 'It's about Andrew and me.' Ah! Marital problems, the sympathetic ear. What could she do but agree?

They meet at a local café on her afternoon off. Once they have ordered, Bridget announces she has made up her mind. She is leaving her husband.

'After eighteen months of psychotherapy I'm ready to go,' Bridget tells her. 'My therapist thinks I'm in great shape.' Bridget sips her coffee. 'I've already found a flat to rent nearby. I can move in next month.'

'And the children? Will they go with you?'

'They'll have to. Andrew can't look after them. He's never home.'

She is impressed by Bridget's resolve, her matter-of-factness in the face of this life-changing event. This must be what Bridget's therapist means by being in great shape. She imagines Bridget's mind as a well-tuned engine, clean and efficient, or hard and sinewy like the body of an athlete. She appears unhampered by guilt or regret, but perhaps that is not true. For all she knows, Bridget might be taking antidepressants and tranquillisers by the fistful, or spend every session with her therapist in floods of tears. Perhaps she is not in good shape at all. But she does not really believe this to be the case. She has counselled too many women in the throes of divorce not to be able to separate the sheep from the goats, the strong from the weak. Bridget, she guesses, has the psychological constitution of an ox.

She is rather surprised that Bridget has asked her to have coffee. Although she has known her for several years through the book club, they have never been particularly close. Bridget's taste in books is decidedly different from hers. There must be many other friends in whom Bridget could confide, so why has she been chosen? Is it possible that Bridget is working her way through the club members, discussing her decision with each woman over coffee or a glass of wine? What number might she be on Bridget's list? Has Bridget sorted women into those with whom she will drink wine and those with whom she will drink coffee? If so, on what basis? She cannot help thinking that coffee-drinking indicates an inferior class of friendship. Or maybe, at this time of sweeping change, Bridget has decided to redefine her friendships: to end those that are no longer workable, to strengthen those that are. If this is the case, then this meeting will have been a wasted exercise. She, for her part, has been unable to strengthen their bond: unable to reach across the table and squeeze Bridget's hand, or to agree that she will be better off out of the marriage. She senses this is what

Bridget wants of her, but how can she comply? What if—in six months, five years—Bridget regrets leaving her husband? She does not want to be implicated in Bridget's decision: she knows too well the repercussions of a decision one comes to regret. In this, as probably in many other things, she cannot be Bridget's ally.

It is time to pick the children up from school. As she walks there she considers another motive for Bridget's phone call. Although it has never been discussed at book club—in her presence, at least: she has made it quite clear that she will not find it helpful—everyone there knows of her court case. Does Bridget see her as a fellow sufferer? She has recognised, for some time now, the parallels between divorce and litigation: the dynamics of guilt and blame, the contract dishonoured, the once powerful brought down by the angry, injured victim. Bridget clearly identifies with the victim, once angry, now empowered, the injured party for whom legal action is the solution, not the problem. Surely Bridget understands the difference in their situations. For all Bridget's talk of right and wrong, can she not see they are on opposing sides?

The boys are already waiting for her at the school gate. As they walk home, Joe takes her hand and tells her about the important events of the day: a playground drama, the model he has made in science class. William walks a few paces ahead. He finds a soft-drink can and kicks it along the concrete footpath, again and again, until she asks him to stop. How will Bridget's children fare, now that the die is cast? And what of her husband?

She has met Andrew briefly, a few times, on the evenings that Bridget has hosted book club. Her impression is that he is not a tyrant, but how can she know what is done, what words are said, when the front door is closed at the end of the evening. What will he do with himself, by himself, on those evenings and weekends his children spend with their mother? That his children, his flesh and blood, are to have a second home, a second life, to which he will be an outsider: will this thought torment him at night, or cause him to drink more than he should? The compartmentalising of lives: lives within lives. If adults find it hard, then how do children manage it? But she is being maudlin, overly dramatic. There are worse things than divorce.

At home she cuts up fruit, spreads peanut butter on biscuits, and gives the children the plate of food to take outside. From the kitchen window she watches them jumping on the trampoline. She would have liked to ask Bridget: *What is the point of no return? What is the point at which the balance irrevocably shifts, so that leaving becomes preferable to staying?* But is it really a question of preference? Shouldn't it be more a question of necessity? Bridget says she feels constrained by her marriage. *But life is shaped by constraints*, she might have countered. *Every aspect of your life calls for a tempering of impulses, a reining-in of self. What degree of constraint, therefore, are you prepared to tolerate? What degree is it necessary to bear?*

The boys come inside, banging the door behind them.

They run past her and down the hall, and the noise of the television blares from the family room. Isn't Bridget concerned that if she stayed a little longer, accepted a little more, or a little less, if she *toughed it out*, the desire to leave might wane? She walks to the family room, finds the remote and turns down the volume. Is she being dispassionate, bloodless to even see things in these terms, to favour the rational over the feelings of the moment? But, after years of being a doctor, how can she not value duty and sacrifice over the feelings of the moment? She does not want to judge Bridget. If the truth be known, in some ways she envies her. While she cannot agree with Bridget's convictions, at least Bridget has the courage to act on them.

'Bridget is leaving her husband,' she tells Paul that evening.

He is reading the newspaper. He does not look up from the page. 'Bridget? Do I know her?'

'No. No, you don't.'

May 11

On Sunday morning Paul takes the boys to visit his parents and she is left alone in the house. After cleaning up the kitchen, she sits down with yesterday's newspaper. She has not read the newspaper for such a long time. In the arts section she comes across an interview with a famous playwright, in which he says he has begun work on a new play. This play is to be about a successful doctor in his fifties who, on becoming disillusioned with his work and his growing detachment from his patients, decides to infect himself with the AIDS virus so that he can connect, through illness and suffering, to the patients he treats.

She puts down the paper and goes to make the beds. This idea of connection through suffering appeals to her now. This playwright has hit on something big, she thinks, something fundamental. The fundamentals of what it is to be human: physical suffering, on the one hand—suffering is the marker of mortality, the precursor of death—and, on the other, the need to love and understand one's fellow human beings and, in turn, to be loved and understood. That the negative force of suffering can have its positive counterbalance in human connection: this idea now appeals to her greatly.

Is she allowed to say, at least to herself, that she has suffered, that she continues to suffer? She is to be punished by Ben Feltham and his band of lawyers, punished for her wrongdoing. Doesn't punishment imply some degree of suffering? But her suffering is not noble. Neither is it blameless. She is denied the privilege of a public, noble suffering. She is no Joan of Arc. Still, she hopes for some recompense in the form of human connection. She hopes that others will sense her suffering—she cannot talk about it, she does not have the right—and understand it. In short, she hopes to be forgiven. She knows she hopes for too much.

As she gathers the washing from the boys' bedroom floor, she wonders at the playwright's choice of illness. The AIDS virus is dramatic enough, almost a character in its own right, but she is not sure the playwright has fully considered the implications of his choice. While community attitudes have somewhat softened over the past twenty years, HIV infection still carries the taint of blame, the stigma of an illness inflicted as a punishment for sinful behaviour. Not, of course, for those children born HIV-positive, or those who contract the illness through a life-saving blood transfusion; that is, those who suffer through no fault of their own. Those infected by such passive means must loudly protest their innocence, or else suffer the shame and suspicion that HIV infection generally confers. Is this what the playwright wants his protagonist to bear? The doctor has infected himself in order to move closer to his patients. She imagines that moment of inoculation; the clinic quiet after hours, the doctor sitting at his desk, a tourniquet tight around his arm, holding the needle poised over an engorged cubital vein. Does he hesitate, the tip of the needle caressing his skin, or does he boldly plunge it in, seeing the blood—his own, as yet uninfected blood—spring back into the barrel of the syringe? But what if the knowledge of his HIV-positive status causes his patients to, instead, move away from him? Will he, too, have to protest his innocence to gain their understanding? Will he have to produce the contaminated syringe, the poisoned needle, as evidence of his blameless route of infection? A needle-stick injury, sustained in the course of duty, he might tell them: that would gain their pity. She does not believe his patients would sympathise, would connect, if they knew he had intentionally infected himself. In order to obtain sympathy and understanding, one must be the victim of the crime, not the perpetrator.

Sitting on William's bed, a pile of dirty washing in her hands, she hears the ticking of the hallway clock and, almost in unison, her own heartbeat pulsing in her ears.

He is a good man, her husband. See how he plays with the children in the garden, bouncing them on the trampoline, shooting hoops through the ring, while she stands at the kitchen window and watches. He is a good man. His children love him. In the evenings they listen for the sound of his key in the front door. 'When will

Dad be home?' they ask her. They need not ask when she will be home because she is always home before them, except on Tuesdays when she works late and Paul picks them up from after-care. Did she marry him for his goodness? Of course she married him for love, but must it be left at that? Love is not above scrutiny: it can be analysed, broken down into its constituent parts. Was her love for him, in part—perhaps in the most part—an appreciation of his goodness? She does not believe that goodness always equates with love. It is possible she could have loved a bad man.

In her work she has encountered many women who profess to love bad men: those men who assault them and abuse their children. *But it is not love you feel*, she could say to these women. For their safety, for their children's safety, she presumes to know what these women feel. *It is fear and self-loathing masquerading as love. Fear, like love, can take many guises. The sense of relief, of reprieve you feel (but you have done nothing wrong, you are not guilty, you should not be punished) when, one night, he does not hit you, does not push your head against a wall, his hands around your throat: be wary of interpreting such relief as a resurgence of love. Do not let relief trick you into forgiveness. The temporary withholding of violence does not equate with kindness.* But she does not say these things.

Instead: 'You must leave with the children. This will take courage but it must be done. Do not accept this as your lot. You and your children deserve better.' She sees the look in these women's eyes as she lectures them on the nature of domestic violence; on depression and social isolation; on self-blame and secrecy.

It is easy for you to say all this, you with your comfortable life, they are thinking. *Words such as yours change nothing.*

My life is not as comfortable as you might think, she could respond. *I, too, have my troubles. I, too, have my persecutors.*

What a joke! She can hear their laughter. *You worry—about what? Your reputation? While we live, every day, in fear of broken bones, or worse? You say you are persecuted? We lie in our beds, each of us waiting, listening to his angry words, his foul words, as he stumbles in the dark outside our rooms, and we ask ourselves: 'How will it be tonight? Will it be us, tonight, or our children?'*

That she, standing at her kitchen window, should think of such things, when all around her is healthy—the green of the garden, her laughing children, her good husband, the clean glass in the kitchen window through which she watches. That she allows herself such black thoughts! The blackest of the black. Once things were as they seem. Now, every scene, every word is false. Things shimmer with symbolic meaning or are distorted beyond recognition. But she has only herself to blame. She has listened to these stories of abuse, shared such awful secrets, not because they have been thrust upon her, but because she has laid herself open to the possibility of such things. In her professional life she has not been afraid to look for suffering when it is hidden. She has seen it as her duty, in some ways her privilege, to open herself to the suffering of others. Did she believe she was immune? How could she have been so foolish, so arrogant as to believe it would all remain outside her; that those words of suffering, once spoken, would cease to exist? It is, has always been, simply a question of time. Now, in her weakened state, the words of those who have suffered have found the break in the integument, the means of entry. Now she cannot shut out those words: like children starved of attention they clamour to be heard so that, watching her husband and her children, hearing their laughter in the sunlit garden, she is brought to thinking of the worst suffering, the darkest cruelty.

How then can her own suffering compare with what she has heard, what she still hears, even as she looks through the window at the sunlight dancing on the leaves? It is as if her own sorrows, her abstract concerns — what is reputation but a puff of air? — are both dwarfed and heightened by those clamouring words. She cannot shut them out. They will be heard. She is bent over at once with suffering and with the shame of it. Better that Paul had been a bad man: then, at least, she would have something inside her worthy of tears.

Sometimes, standing at the sink, her hands steeped in warm water, or outside in the garden, examining a plant at close quarters, she finds herself asking if she still loves him, or if, in fact, it matters either way. It is not so much a question of whether there is *love* between them — even this is an absurd assertion, as if love were somehow a thing of substance, visible and quantifiable, or a constant, like a mathematical coefficient, when she knows love to wax and wane like the moon—but rather whether there is more to be gained from being together than from being apart. This, of course, can never be truly determined: the experience of one state precludes the other. There is no opportunity for a double-blind, randomised controlled trial. And by what criteria, what yardstick can total gains be measured? By one's level of happiness? No measurement is more unreliable and subjective. The only objective criterion that can be used, she believes, is financial status. Everything else being equal, one is financially better off staying married.

She knows this analysis, were she ever to express it to others, would be viewed as cynical. She prefers to think of it as clinical: a clinical assessment of the signs and symptoms of the married condition. While the word 'clinical' is currently out of favour—one thinks of its negative connotations: cold, metal surfaces; starched, white coats; the smell of antiseptic—she does not mean to be cold. She wants only to be honest, to faithfully record the signs (Paul no longer kisses her when he leaves for work, they seldom have sex) and symptoms (the tears that fall of their own accord, the tightness in her chest when she hears his key in the front door) of their ailing marriage. As a doctor of twenty years, she had seen herself as inured to illness. She now feels both hardened and vulnerable.

May 12

Now that she is aware of her disfigurement, it is more difficult to smile. In the past smiling has involved the stretching of the lips away from the teeth so that the gum line is revealed. Now, if she is to smile an open smile it must only be a half-smile, so that the lips still cover the gums. A closed smile is safer—although it makes her look bored or smug—for she can never be quite sure how much is revealed once she shows any part of her teeth. But perhaps it is preferable to stop smiling at all. Smiling uses more facial muscles than any other expression, and with facial expressions come expression lines. At forty-three, a woman must think of such things. She will save her smiles for her children and their friends who come to play; she does not want her children's friends to think of her as stern. As for the rest, she will maintain impassivity: she will show them all a face of stone.

'I know you are worried,' Paul says to her that evening, as she examines her mouth in the bathroom mirror. 'But you shouldn't let this take over. There are other things that need your attention.'

'Such as?'

'Such as the children.'

'Are you saying I neglect the children?'

'Not in a day-to-day sense. It's just that sometimes you seem ... cut off.'

'I'm doing the best I can. I have a lot to deal with. I don't think you understand just how difficult things are.'

'I understand how stressful the case must be—at least, I'm trying to understand what that's like for you. But this other matter of your teeth: I think you're worrying too much about something that is ultimately not going to cause you any serious problems.'

'Are you going to tell me that things could be worse? That I could have cancer instead?'

'Well, it's true.'

'Yes, it's true. I could have an osteosarcoma. Or I could have a son with it.'

It is no longer a question of whether she is a good mother, although at one time, when William was born, she had doubted her capacity. At that time it was something she had never done before. She was not used to taking on new roles, increased responsibilities, without some prior training. Now she is not so concerned with the practice of motherhood according to the letter of the law. She now knows, with respect to the daily tasks of mothering, what to do, what not to do. She is proficient enough. But she is not the mother she once thought she would be; that is, at a time before she had children of her own. As a child she had most admired those mothers who were physically demonstrative, those ample-bosomed women who called her *sweetheart* and put an arm around her shoulder as they talked, or kissed her goodnight when she slept over. While she may not have been the type of child to invite hugs and kisses, she was happy, very happy to receive them from those women who had plenty to give; who seemed, even from her child's view, to thrive on giving. She still meets women like this.

But, according to the letter of the law, no one can accuse her of being a bad mother. She performs the tasks of mothering—making the lunches, labelling the clothes, supervising piano practice—but the tasks are infinite: why try to list them? Yet she performs them in a way that does not, in her eyes at least, seem motherly. She ticks off the tasks in her head—a checklist, like the many she learned in medical school. She is motivated by love of a dutiful kind, rather than a bounteous, joyous love that bursts its seams and flows into every room of the house.

But her two boys. She waits for them at the school gate. As she watches them come towards her, she marvels at how their hair shines in the sun, how their skin glows with life. Of all the mothers standing at the school gate, she is proud to be the one to love her children's hair, so thick and straight, her children's skin that glows with health. Can its absence of blemish be attributed to her in some way? Of course she has been vigilant with sunscreen and hats but she is thinking more of the essential goodness of their skin: can she take some of the credit for that? Is it wrong to want some of the credit for their goodness?

Her mother phones to tell her that a long-time family friend has multiple myeloma. 'He says there is no cure for it,' her mother says. 'Is that true?'

Of course her mother wants to believe her friend will be cured. It is only natural. She does not want to dash her mother's hopes. She remembers her mother's friend fondly. He has children her own age, several grandchildren. She, too, would like to see him better, but good wishes do not mitigate the course of a disease. 'There is the possibility of remission,' she says to her mother. 'He may have many good years yet.'

She puts down the phone. Her ear aches from pressing too hard against the receiver. Too hard and too long. She is sick of listening, of taking things in. Although she might appear to be, she is not a hollow vessel. People spill their troubles, pour out their hearts to her. All those tears, that liquid suffering must go somewhere. There are days she feels full to the brim, ready to burst with the pressure of it all. Perhaps if she talked, did a little outpouring herself, she would fell less full. She sees the words gushing from her mouth, the tears streaming down her face, feels the heaving of her heart as her words flow in torrents. *I have done something wrong, something very bad. A young man has lost his leg, partly because* — but always this need to qualify! — *because of what I have done or, rather, failed to do.* To whom can she say these things? Paul cannot be her vessel. He is implicated in the telling: her stream of thoughts would eventually turn to him. She might say to her patients: *I understand your work is causing you distress, but, tell me, in the course of your daily employment, have you ever had cause to feel responsible for the loss of another person's limb?* They would think her mad, yet she would only be telling the truth.

Should she seek counselling? How she hates that word. She has thought, many times, of therapy; the quiet room, the upholstered armchair into which she will sink, a box of tissues within reach. But a psychiatrist! *Spare me your transference and counter-transference, your wooden, defensive silence. This is an affair of the heart. Do not pretend that Freud and Lacan can help.* They would tear her story from her and give her nothing to replace it.

At work, passing David in the corridor, there have been moments of temptation, but she has always held herself back. She must think of what will be achieved by yielding to impulses. David will listen, she has no doubt of that. He will usher her into his room and listen, regarding her with kind, liquid eyes; nodding his square head thoughtfully, sympathetically, as, of course, he must. How else could he behave? She cannot bear the thought of his sympathy. *Weak, silly woman!* he will think as she blathers on. *Get a grip, move on. You made a mistake. Make amends and move on. Move on, move on.* Always this sense of being urged forwards, the firm hand in the small of her back, when what she wants to do is turn around and return to a place where she could utter a sentence or walk across a room without fear of doing wrong. If she talks to David, if she *unburdens herself,* he will insist she takes time off; *to rest and recover,* he will say, his hand on her shoulder. *She is a complete mess, not fit to work,* he will tell others, behind her back. He will expect her, at some date, as yet unspecified, to return to work, hale and hearty. *Recovery is not always guaranteed, David.* Remissions and relapses are the best she can hope for. But if she leaves now she will never return. Her only chance of survival is to cling to the side of the boat. She hopes she can cling tight. She hopes that the flood of tears, the downpour of sorrows will not be strong enough to wash her away.

May 13

They have fallen into a night-time routine, one she believes to be mutually satisfactory. As soon as the boys have gone to bed Paul goes to the study to work. She retires to the couch, wrapped in her dressing-gown — the thick blue gown that Paul has never liked — and watches television. She has developed quite a taste for medical dramas: the esoteric diagnoses, the hospital romances.

When watching television her adrenaline surges — it is as if she were there — as an unconscious patient is wheeled through the doors from the ambulance bay and descended upon by the emergency team. These doctors and nurses are cool under pressure, performing complex procedures — inserting an intrathoracic drain tube, a central venous line — with speed and precision. They are all action and decisiveness, seemingly infallible, but, in those moments when the emergency has passed and the camera lingers in close-up, their vulnerability is evident as they stand in the doorway of the treatment room, on the threshold of revelation, with a quivering lip or tears in their eyes. In their white coats and surgical garb it is difficult to believe they are actors. Yet what real doctor is ever as capable and caring, as endowed with such attractive human frailties as those on the screen? Certainly none she has ever met.

She now wishes she had trained in a speciality that was more cut and dried: anaesthetics, for instance, or emergency medicine. She is tired of the negotiation of general practice. *How do you feel about that?* she must ask of each patient. *Tell me the pros and cons as you see them*. It is a wonder she gets anything done. But an anaesthetist need not negotiate with an unconscious patient. An emergency physician, when faced with a patient in ventricular fibrillation, does not weigh the arguments for and against defibrillation. Instead, the paddles are immediately placed on the chest and *wham!* Two hundred joules delivered though the chest wall to the patient's heart. She sees it all now, just as it is on television. Then, as the patient's body jolts from the electric charge—the back arching so that the upper body lifts off the bed then slumps back down, the arms flailing behind—the emergency physician, in his crisp white coat, his eyes narrowed, his jaw set, watches the cardiac monitor. The camera focuses on the path of the green line across the monitor. Is it back into sinus rhythm? Then she can breathe a sigh of relief. Is it a single flat line? *Zap him again*, she urges her television counterpart. In the midst of a cardiac arrest, the biopsychosocial model does not apply. Instead, all is biological: the electrical rhythm of the damaged heart, the concentration of potassium in the blood, the degree of oxygenation of the tissues.

Such parameters are eminently quantifiable and, being quantifiable, have discrete limits of normality. Indecision, hesitancy and delayed response are the cardinal sins of emergency medicine. When a life hangs in the balance, every decision is absolute.

How, then, can general practice compare? Much of her daily work is mundane and repetitive. The patient with hypertension has his blood pressure measured at every visit, ad nauseam, from time of diagnosis to time of death, although now what relief she feels when a patient comes for a blood-pressure check. All she need do is record the figure and, if it is acceptable, renew the prescription and review in six months: a simple reflex exercise. She has lost interest in spending those last-available minutes in asking her hypertensive patient about diet or exercise, as she used to, so conscientiously. Instead, she takes those last few minutes, alone at her desk, to gather herself, to steel herself for the next encounter. She used to give her time so readily. Now she hungrily guards it for herself.

It is the continuing care, the hallmark of her profession, she has come to dread the most. Her patients with chronic illnesses—osteoarthritis, diabetes—come to her again and again, at each visit putting their care back into her hands. Her hands are now too unsteady, unfit for the task. Like a closet alcoholic, she shakes and stumbles with her patients, while, with a wooden smile, she pretends all is as it was. Like the bottle tucked inside a drawer, the mint under the tongue to mask the liquored breath, she hides from them her secret sin, her downfall. She should come clean. If she had the courage, she would nail a declaration to the front door: *Doctor McBride is on trial for negligence. Take heed and enter at your own risk.* She cannot do it.

The course of chronic illness is unfailingly downhill. With osteoarthritis come the first twinges of pain, the flurry of diagnosis that later settles into the gradual onset of daily disability, the growing list of failed treatment modalities. A patient with newly diagnosed diabetes is intrigued by the novelty of blood-glucose measurements, the sleek glucometer that flashes and beeps, and inspired by the notion of lifestyle change—surely the chrysalis can change into a butterfly? When the low-fat diet, the walks around the park fail to deliver or fail to eventuate, oral agents are required. Years later, still visiting the doctor but, despite the glucometer readings, despite the ever-increasing doses of medication, despite everyone's best intentions, insulin injections become the mainstay of treatment. Insulin, infection and impotence, silent myocardial infarction and death: at each step, a decision to be made. So many decisions for so many patients: doesn't it follow that some are bound to be wrong? She thinks now that, with each patient treated, an emergency physician has a single opportunity to err. General practitioners, over years of consultations with any given patient, have so many.

She is surprised by how easily her thinking has changed. It is as if the template of her previous beliefs and attitudes has been simply reversed, so that what was once cut away, in shadow, has now been thrown into relief. She had always seen her role as one of illness prevention and health maintenance; now she sees herself watching, helpless with indecision, as her patients shuffle, day by day, year by year, inexorably towards the cliff's edge. Where once she saw life she now sees death.

May 14

It is possible to live with someone and yet live a solitary life. Of course one can feel alone in a crowd, but she has also found it easy, surprisingly easy, to be physically alone when at home. It can be done subtly, almost seamlessly: the leaving of a room soon after he enters. Not storming out—she does not want an argument—but trying to create an impression of leaving with the purpose of doing something else in another room. She can be cooking, quite legitimately, in the kitchen, while he reads a book in the living room. She can supervise the boys' homework in the family room while he makes a phone call from the study—a long call with the door closed. As she walks past the study door she sometimes hears him laugh. Together they have designed their home to have private spaces, communal spaces, family spaces for family life. How lucky she was to marry an architect! They have spent many Saturdays together, the boys in tow, choosing furniture and appliances. They have sat together for hours discussing the colour of the walls and bathroom tiles, samples and colour charts spread around them, a panoply of choice.

The possibilities were once endless.

At the dinner table it is easy to direct conversation to the children, to reprimand them on their table manners; in this way conversation of sorts is procured without the necessity of addressing him directly. She will not have silence. What will come from it? Dinner is usually quick: she does not linger at the table. There are always things to be done after dinner.

She spends more time in the garden, pulling up weeds, pruning branches—she is most content in the farthest corners, the most overgrown areas, where she is hidden from view. The marriage bed is more difficult territory. She can go to bed earlier or later than he, but only up to a point; sooner or later she must meet him in bed. But even this, this physical meeting, can be undertaken without too much confrontation. Sometimes she leaves a room just as he enters: both of them turning sideways in the doorway so as to let the other pass, so physically close, a body's width between them, but like strangers, distantly polite, unable to meet each other's eye. The choreography of evasion. These are terrible moments.

From the foreshore, where now she often walks, she sees cargo ships anchored in the bay. She does not know why they moor there for hours, even days at a time; perhaps the port is full and they must wait their turn to unload. At night the ships, so plain and utilitarian by day, are lit up so that they resemble holiday cruisers. Standing on the foreshore at dusk, she almost expects to hear laughter, strains of music, the clink of glasses drift across the water. She knows the ships are too far away for such sounds to reach her—and, besides, they carry cargo, not holidaying passengers—but her expectation is raised by their romantic night-time appearance; festooned with lights, anchored on the darkening water, having come from some exotic place—Vladivostok, perhaps, or Shanghai—and soon to go back there. She often returns the next day to find the ship gone, the journey resumed. She has become strangely fond of them, these cargo ships that float on the bay, large and sturdy, like giant tethered beasts. From time to time she brings a pair of binoculars with her and reads the lettering on the hull.

She taunts Paul now, although he does not seem to know it. As a wronged wife, isn't it her right to occasionally be cruel? Has she been wronged, she sometimes wonders? The evidence is only circumstantial. But there are other ways of knowing. She need not rely on forensic proof: the lipstick on the collar is not her modus operandi. Over dinner she questions him about his day at work. 'Who did you work with today?' 'Where did you have lunch?' Or, on the nights he is later home than usual: 'Where have you been?' She need not mention her name. She leaves that up to him. 'Kate is working with me on an apartment block in the city,' he might say. 'Kate and I had a two-hour meeting with the client this afternoon.'

Got you! she thinks, but she is less than triumphant. She watches him as he utters her name (the softly guttural *k*, the *t* formed with the tip of his tongue), examining him for the telltale signs of arousal: the dilation of his pupils, the catch in his voice, the heightened colour that begins at his throat and spreads upward to his face, an increase in his respiratory rate. She would look for other signs, definitive signs of male arousal, if she could do so undetected. And why not? If he has betrayed her with his body then why not subject his body to her powers of observation? *I have powers you do not know of*, she thinks as she watches him across the dinner table. *I have been trained to watch and listen. I have been watching you for twenty years.*

She decides to take up knitting. She has not knitted since she was a teenager, when she made herself a Fair-Isle jumper in cream-coloured eight-ply. But, of an evening, when there is nothing else to do, she finds knitting to be a suitable pastime. It can be relaxing, the *click-click* of the needles, the motion of the wool as it loops and slips around her index finger. She would like to make the boys each a jumper, but they would not wear them, so instead she is knitting herself a cardigan in soft, brown mohair. She likes, at the end of an evening's work, to measure her progress; to see how much the sleeve has lengthened, how close she is to casting off. Paul sometimes leaves the study and sits down beside her to scan through the newspaper. They sit without speaking, the silence only broken by the clicking of her needles or the rustling of his newspaper as he turns the page. Is this the language they now speak to each other? The language of self-absorption and indifference? But she is not indifferent. It would be easier if she were. She looks only at her knitting, laying it flat on the sofa and running her hand over the soft length of wool, or at the instructions in the pattern book—two purl, two plain—while inside she is aware of a shaking, like that of the rumbling of an earthquake deep beneath the surface. If she could but erupt! If she could only scream and punch, claw at his face and pull his hair, while he catches her by her flailing wrists and smothers her face in kisses. With a sigh, perhaps for the state of world affairs, he folds the paper and leaves the room. She puts her hand to the place where, for a while, he sat: it is still warm but cools quickly. She packs up her knitting and goes to bed.

It is three weeks since they have had sex. Never before has there been such an abstinence, not since they met that December night in the hallway of a Carlton terrace: he, dressed in black, his hair falling across his face; she in her dress of full-blown roses. He had walked her home, past the cemetery, his arm around her shoulder. Against the cemetery wall they had kissed. Their first kiss, in the realm of the dead. Had it been, all along, a terrible omen?

Even after the boys were born they did not wait three weeks. She remembers the first time after William's birth: how tender Paul had been, yet all she could think about was her baby, sleeping just an arm's length away. Afterwards she had whispered *family* in Paul's ear, feeling for the first time the weight of the word: its joy, its safety, its portent.

She does not want to think about why it has not happened, is not inclined to list the opportunities that were let slip away: any such analysis will involve some apportioning of blame. Three weeks, give or take a day. How easily a habit of twenty years is broken. Paul would be irritated by the notion of habit, but she is all too aware of the well-worn grooves into which their sex life has settled. She has not minded. She is not fiery or passionate by nature: her appetites are modest. Well-worn grooves can be comforting. But three weeks! Could it be that they will never have sex again? Is the memory of sex all that remains? She is already nostalgic, recalling fragmented images: the fold of the sheet against his thigh ... She searches for visual cues but they do not come. Neither are sensations specific: the frictions of membrane, skin and tongue she cannot recall with any precision. What, then, remains? Only the knowledge that she was once a woman who had sex with her husband because, at one time, it was what they both wanted.

She knows of some women, some of her older patients, who have been happy to end their days of lovemaking, trading sex for the seclusion of a single bed. After years of child-rearing and appeasing their husbands, these women view the termination of sex as a hard-earned right. But she is not of their age, not of their culture—she cannot absolve herself so easily. How would it be if she and Paul were to have sex again, perhaps tonight? They would be as awkward as a pair of teenagers but with none of the hope and passion. There would be nothing new about it. The act would be heavy with the weight of the preceding three weeks: the silences, borne of anger and sadness, the slipping away of habit and, alongside it, love. The habit of love can so easily be broken. In lovemaking there is often embedded a kernel of hate, waiting, like orgasm, to be released. Can anyone really lay themselves bare? Perhaps, three weeks ago, quietly and without forewarning—the act hasty and half-hearted at the end of a desultory day—they arrived at the point of no return. There must be such a point for every couple: the one last congress before death, of one kind or another. Would it have been better to have known? She might have marked the occasion in some memorable way. She might have bathed and anointed herself with fragrant oils—musky, dank-scented oils that hinted at dark secrets—and, at the point of climax, she might have whispered in his ear: *This is the last time. Do not ever forget it.*

There are practicalities to consider. She does not know how to hang a door or use a power drill. At a pinch, she could change a tyre: she has done this before, but long ago, when her time was her own. Changing a tyre by herself—the positioning of the jack, the dry gritty feel of the rubber as she lifted the spare from the boot—was once a challenge to be savoured. She is sick of challenges. Sick and tired. She had once thought she was a feminist, but if she ever were, she is no longer. What feminist worth her salt would shy away from such things? If she is to ever live alone, she will live not as a female warrior, armed with nail gun and leather apron, but as an old maid, withering in her parlour, the doors rotting on their hinges and the roof caving in around her.

May 15

She has begun to wake at night to the sound of footsteps in the hallway. Sometimes the sound is more like the swish of a long skirt on the floorboards, outside the bedroom door. Is it that, on the edge of wakefulness, she dreams these sounds? Or could these be some sort of auditory hallucinations? Is she, in fact, slipping into psychosis? She used not to believe in ghosts. Now it is hard to know what to believe. The house is more than one hundred years old: old enough to have its secrets, its restless spirits, if one is to believe in such things. She lies awake, waiting for the sound of a wooden leg tapping the floor, a footfall and then a *tap*, the pattern of sound (footfall and *tap*, footfall and *tap*) moving ever closer, for this is how retribution will come: in the dead, the blackness of night. All at once her heart hammers in her chest, so hard it feels as if it will burst through her sternum. Her breathing comes quick and shallow, her forehead and palms grow wet with sweat. She hears herself panting, *like an animal*, she thinks. *This is panic. You know what to do*. But her body has other ideas. *Fight or flee*, it tells her. *Stand up and fight your ghost or run for your life. Dead boys have wings so you must run fast.* But Ben Feltham is not dead, she reminds herself as she struggles to draw breath. At least, he is not dead yet. Who knows if and when the secondary tumours will surface, like bobbing apples, in his lungs? And he will not come limping on a wooden leg. Wooden legs are a thing of the past, a thing of nightmares. He will come on crutches, made of aluminium, the ends stoppered with rubber, his left pants leg folded and pinned neatly behind, or he will wear a prosthetic limb, skilfully fashioned from fibreglass and plastic, so that the unevenness in his footfall will be barely heard.

He was once an athlete, a cross-country runner. She wrote it in his file, on that first visit: *Left knee pain after 5km run.* Such a simple observation of cause and effect and, yet, so brutally misguided. *You were arrogant enough to assume the running caused the pain?* the prosecuting barrister will ask of her some day, maybe soon. *Did you think to ask about night-time pain?* How his voice will echo around that courtroom! How will she bear it?

He was once an athlete but now he is a cripple, limping on a stump of bone, the skin tucked around it like a puckered mouth. Does he understand that this ruche of skin, this lump of scarred flesh, is now his most-valued possession? Damage or neglect the skin of his stump and he cannot wear a prosthesis, cannot pretend to be other than he is. She would do it all for him, if he would only let her. She would be his nurse, his valet. Each night, while he sat on his bed, she would examine his stump under the bedside lamp, peering closely at the rippled flesh. Any sign of a pressure sore would cause her distress. She would wash the stump gently with warm soapy water and dry it carefully with the softest of towels. In the mornings she would be there to help him as he dressed, covering his stump with a clean, dry sock that she would then smooth free of creases. All this she would do, and more besides, to protect him from the ravages of dirt and sweat. (That a young man who once won long-distance races, once tackled in the mud of the football field, must now be fearful of dirt and sweat. That this is her doing.)

Does he know that she thinks of him often? Each morning, as he straps his false leg to his body, does he sense her concern? If, one night, she sees him hovering at her bedside she will tell him so. Before he puts the pillow to her face she will wish him good health, long life. She was once his doctor. It is a hard habit to break.

May 20

In the evening, on her way home from work, she takes a detour along the beach road. It is just past dusk. She turns off the road into a foreshore parking bay and gets out of her car. The foreshore path is deserted. The overhead lamps along the path illuminate the sand, groomed and clean. Beyond this patchy light lies the sea, dark and solid. There is no breeze to stir the waves, no white water against the black. She leaves the parking bay and walks along the path to a small grassy rise overlooking the beach. She climbs halfway up the hill to a bench seat, where she sits for a while in the gathering dark, watching the lights of the cargo ships far out to sea.

With a noisy beating of wings, a flock of white birds —probably seagulls, although she cannot clearly make them out—is suddenly airborne, travelling westward across the bay. It seems late in the day for birds to be flying, but perhaps they need not fly far. Their nesting place might be nearby: under the pier, in the nooks and crannies of the creaking crossbeams, or in one of the scraggly she-oaks that line the foreshore.

Then, against the water, something luminous catches

her eye, moving from left to right across her field of vision. For a moment she thinks it is a phosphorescent water creature, skimming the water's surface with one magnificent flying leap; a flying fish with an elaborate dorsal fin, or, stranger still, a rare aquatic creature of the dinosaur age. She waits for it to submerge, but it stays above the water, continuing its steady path, and she comes to realise it is only a bird, flying close to the sea, the faint light from the land reflecting on its outstretched wings. On the horizon the ships wink blue and red, talking to each other.

May 22

She should go to the awards dinner, or perhaps she should not. Paul has not yet asked if she is going with him. Does his silence stem from concern for her, for *her big day* next week, *her day in court*? Or instead does it come from his wish, his ardent wish, that she stay at home and leave him to his own devices?

That is how things are now: between the mentioning and the doing, between talk and action, there are a million permutations and combinations of presumption and suspicion, fear and longing, hurt and regret. She could go to the dinner for Paul's sake, or equally for his sake stay home. It is not that her decision is arbitrary. Whether she goes or not will depend not on her whim—there is no such thing these days—but, instead, on the spirit in which she goes. If she can muster enough strength, for strength is what it will take, then she will go in a supportive spirit. If not, if the day, *her big day*, has been difficult, more difficult than she had ever imagined, it will be better for Paul that she stays home. Everything is a day-to-day proposition. She can offer no more than that.

'You haven't said anything about the awards dinner,' she says to him that night as he is cleaning his teeth. 'You haven't asked if I am coming.'

He turns to her while he continues brushing, the toothpaste foaming in his mouth. His toothbrush moves in neat circular movements from top to bottom, side to side. A perfectly normal domestic scene: a husband and wife sharing the bathroom before bed and yet, at this moment, it is as if she were watching a stranger cleaning his teeth. She feels the blood rise to her cheeks. She should never have mentioned it. She should never have shown her hand.

May 23

She is in the kitchen eating lunch when David enters carrying a lunch box, a general-practice tabloid tucked under his arm. It is the first time she has seen him today. He greets her with a mock salute: two fingers briefly to his temple, almost as if he were miming the act of a gun to the head. He draws a chair into the table, opens his lunch box and takes out a sandwich wrapped in plastic. He peels away the plastic wrap and the smell of canned tuna and onion fills the room.

'How was your morning?' he asks her, his elbows propped on the table, holding the sandwich delicately in both hands.

'Not bad,' she replies cautiously. 'Not too busy.' Her appointment schedule used to be fully booked every day, usually three or four days in advance. Now there are one or two vacant appointments every session. She has taken to repeatedly checking the appointment diary on the computer and wondering, as she stares at the blank spaces on the screen, who they might be, these one or two patients in twelve who have changed their minds about her competence. She has tried to make herself see this in a positive light, to feel reassured by the presence of the other ten patients who phone the clinic and ask particularly for her. Of course, on any given day, she might also be the only doctor to have vacancies. The doctor of last resort: she has considered this possibility, too.

'And you? How's your morning been?' She feels obliged to ask.

David has a mouthful of sandwich, so cannot answer immediately. Instead he nods in time to the vertical movement of his jaw, his expression serious, as if he is thinking deeply about her question. His sandwich is brimming with goodness: wholemeal bread, thickly cut and filled with mixed lettuce leaves, grated carrot, the unmistakeable crimson stain of beetroot.

'I saw an interesting rash today,' David says finally. 'Guttate psoriasis, I think. The history fits: fourteen-year-old boy, recent sore throat. Quite classic, really.' He takes another bite of his sandwich and she watches his cheeks fill with food. She finds herself irritated by his eating—the deliberate, ordinary movements of his mouth and pharynx—and by the total lack of self-consciousness he conveys, sitting over his plastic lunch box, unapologetic despite the lingering smell of tuna, his eyes straying to the front page of the medical newspaper. She has known him twelve years. He is only two years her senior but has always seemed much older. He is in all respects a thoroughly decent person; a good family man, sensible and sane: methodical, yes, but, in medical terms, there is nothing wrong with that. She could never brand him an egotist and yet, at this moment, she finds his smugness infuriating. Why did he not invite her in to see the boy's rash? Was her opinion not worth seeking?

'Margaret tells me you're not working next Wednesday,' David says. 'Is everything all right?' He looks at her and she feels herself blush.

'It's the mediation meeting. I'm sure I told you about it.'

'Mediation is next week?' He puts down his sandwich and crosses his forearms, resting them on the table. 'Then why don't you take Monday and Tuesday off as well? Have some time to prepare.'

She attempts a smile. 'It's not an exam, David. I don't need to cram. Besides, I've been preparing for three years now.'

'I didn't mean it in that way.'

'No, of course not.' She is evading his questioning look, evading his concern and he must know it. But she does not want to hear about—not from him, anyway—the mental-health benefits of yoga or meditation, or the breathing exercises she might employ as she enters the County Court building and takes the lift to the third floor. Why should she become David's patient? If he were in her shoes, she would not expect that of him.

David rewraps the remainder of his sandwich and takes an apple from the lunch box. 'You know that if at any time you want to take time off or cut back your sessions, you need only say the word.'

'And which word is that? Breakdown? Acopia?' She

means to be flippant but finds she cannot keep the shrillness from her voice.

He does not smile. 'You are managing incredibly well —we've all remarked on that.'

Somehow he makes it feel like a criticism. Would he have preferred that she come to him in floods of tears?

'Nevertheless, it must be hard. I just want to reassure you that taking time off is fine with me—and with Rohan, for that matter—so don't feel you can't, as far as the practice is concerned.'

'Time off won't change what has happened, and I can't see the point of just sitting at home.' *Is that what you would do in my situation?* she wants to ask him. *Sit at home and chew your nails?* But it is not his situation. It is hers. 'Better, I think, that I just get on with things.'

After this they sit in silence. No longer able to finish her lunch, she flips through a magazine. David goes to the sink, opens the cutlery drawer and trawls though it. The sound of the clanging metal sets her teeth on edge. He returns to the table with a vegetable knife and begins to peel his apple. She watches, despite herself, as it seems—can it be so?—he is trying to ensure the strand of apple peel does not break. A continuous strand, as David's life has been, at least what she knows of it: from his suburban boys' private school to a place, comfortably gained, at the University of Melbourne. The six years of medical school he would have seen as cumulative, knowledge building on knowledge, the disparate threads of knowledge—anatomy, pharmacology, human physiology—interweaving and strengthening with every year. Did he ever question his commitment to knowledge? Was he ever afraid that anatomical and physiological fact would fail to be enough, would ultimately disappoint?

He finishes peeling the apple and the thin ribbon of peel, spiralling in on itself, falls to the table, unbroken. She has always viewed his style of medical practice as different from hers: the cut-and-dried versus the more intuitive approach. Evidence-based medicine could not have a truer disciple than David. Different styles, but complementary. Different but, nonetheless, equal: the male–female divide. Does he now look at her and see his approach vindicated? Perhaps he regards, has always regarded, her intuitive approach as simply an excuse for a disorganised filing system, or a poor memory for protocol. Would he, given her situation, have done better? Would things have been different if she were like him?

May 25

What dreams she has! Florid and tortured, etched into her waking brain. She has no need of a therapist: she can interpret them herself.

She has dreamed she comes home to find a woman in the house with Paul. The woman is tall and fat, tearful and vulnerable, with compressed lips, a receding chin. Paul will not explain why the woman is there; he mumbles, he looks away. Again she returns home to find Paul dressed in a bizarre costume: an embroidered Tyrolean jacket and leather sandals, a large white rose pinned to his lapel. The fat woman is by his side, sheathed in red, her compressed lips bright with crimson lipstick. Paul tells her he is marrying this woman. *Why?* she asks. *Because of the love she gives to me and to the children. I need love and she gives it. The children need love, too.* In the dream she is lost for words but as she wakes, the answer comes: *You are right. Of course you are right.*

She has dreamed Paul has a mistress and everyone knows it. This woman, of Scandinavian appearance—lean, muscular limbs; white-blonde hair tied in a smooth, swinging ponytail; blue eyes; flawless skin—is heavily pregnant with his child. This, too, is common knowledge. Who is to say that in reality such a thing would not happen? She is on the stage of a vast, empty theatre. She stands in the shadows, waiting in the wings, while Paul and his mistress take centrestage. It seems they are both bathed in a dazzling white light but it could be that the light comes from the woman herself, from her glowing skin, her shining hair, from her foetus that churns and brims with life. Somehow she knows they are having a boy. (But *she* has already given Paul two sons: no one can say she has not done what was required. Not that she knows what is required: no one has ever spelled it out. But bearing children—two healthy sons—must be somewhere high on the list.)

In her dream, although she stands hidden from view, she knows Paul and his mistress are aware of her presence. She knows, too, they feel no shame, no need to hide from her their nakedness. Besides, they have eyes only for each other. They are consumed by each other. So she stands and watches, as Paul kneels to stroke the voluptuous belly of his pregnant mistress. He leans his head against her belly, its protuberance accentuated by her leanness, so that she seems all belly, all light, as she rests her hands upon his shoulders. Such a private, joyous moment and yet she need not turn away. She knows she is required to watch. It is her penance to look upon her husband in the throes of his passion, to see him consumed, body and soul, by another woman, more beautiful, more luminous than she could ever, ever be. In her dream she feels no anger, no sense of injustice: instead the heavy detachment of the sinner who, for one brief moment, is allowed to witness perfection.

This dream! Such stagy melodrama, such clichéd pathos! Yet she can only say this long after she has shaken off her waking state and wiped away her tears.

There is another dream, too, that recurs in obsessively fixed detail. She is in the boys' bedroom. She kisses them as they sleep: Joe first, then William. *My boys, my boys*, she whispers. She walks twelve steps—always twelve—along the hallway. The clock strikes three as she passes. She pauses outside her and Paul's bedroom door, her hand on the doorknob, but does not enter. She waits only long enough to hear the creak of the bedsprings, a sigh of expiration, then she opens the front door and leaves the house. In the dream she is empty-handed, bare-footed. As the door closes behind her, the dream always ends.

May 26

Her patients are real, flesh and blood, authentic in body and mind. Even their evasions, their attempts at concealment, their denials have an honesty, an earthy substantiveness that soothes her, holds her up when she is about to fall. Is this something to do with predictability? Is there something about the predictability, the commonality of the people she sees that authenticates them in her eyes? Is it enough to see this commonality in others, to recognise it and be held up by it, when one is about to fall? Now, each time she places the stethoscope over a patient's chest, each time she inserts the scalpel blade through a patient's skin, she is reassured by the predictability of what she finds: the muffled sounds of a beating heart, its rhythm sometimes regular, sometimes not, yet beating all the same; the way in which the skin springs back from the path of the knife, a myriad of tiny vessels bleeding in its wake. The predictability of flesh and function is now what sustains her. And also, perhaps, what sets her apart. If she were to draw the scalpel blade across her own flesh, what would she uncover, once the dermis was breached? Would she bleed as her patients do, would the fluid that seeped from *her* veins reassure her of her own humanity?

She has become concerned with appearance: the appearance of competence rather than the substance of it. The substance she can fix up later: she can check the textbook or the pharmacopoeia, make a call to a colleague, after the patient has left the room, in that hiatus, that quiet time, when one patient has left and the next has not yet entered. But it is the *appearance* of competence that must be maintained in the here and now of the consultation, the patient seated in front of her, watching her, so that all goes smoothly, so that the patient does not detect anything untoward. While she listens to a patient she also gauges the atmosphere of the room, she *sniffs it out*, attempting to determine if her appearance is still intact, if she has *got away with it*. But she has not got away with it: she has already been discovered. She has now learned that patients, when speaking, are more concerned with themselves and their stories, their individual tales of woe, than with the doctor, so long as the doctor listens attentively and does not try to brush them off or to trivialise in any way the importance of their story. It is only when the doctor speaks that patients begin to look outwards, to judge the one who speaks. Now, as *she* speaks, she is aware they look at her; not just that their eyes rest on her features but that they look critically, assessing what she says according to certain criteria: *Does what this doctor says accord with my*

*own interpretation of the problem? Is this doctor telling me
things I do not want to hear? Does this doctor even know what
she is talking about?* As she is speaking, explaining her
diagnosis and management, sketching diagrams of the
middle ear, the kidney — these diagrams are too small,
too inadequate, she presses too hard with the pen, going
over and over the same detail, drawing arrows, too many
arrows, to indicate the changes in pressure, the direction
of flow, to label anatomical features — she sees through
their eyes her own face; sees her own features set into a
grimace, a frown; sees how her features lack spontaneity,
seem awkward and frozen, as if she has a facial palsy. The
young women are the worst. They watch her with eyes
that say: *You are faltering, crumbling. You are getting old.*

Her words are coming back to haunt her. She means no
one any ill will: isn't that true? Yet she is horrified by
what she says to her patients. As a doctor she is forever
filtering words: when opening the consultation she has
been taught not to ask *How are you?* but instead *How
can I help you today?* Such a presumption! She does not
always help. The filtering of words grows more and more
difficult as it becomes increasingly necessary. She thinks
of a sieve, such as the boys once used when panning for
gold in a stream: the mesh of the sieve becoming ever
more clogged with silt, the draining of water around the
stones becoming ever slower. She filters the patient's
words as well as her own: she translates their words into
medical language, discarding those words and phrases that

are superfluous to diagnosis, those words that need no translation. When speaking to patients, she has avoided brutal terms—cancer, amputation, death—diluting bad news with a surfeit of information—referrals, treatments, side effects, support groups: there is always so much to say when avoiding the unsayable. She has filtered her words, not to obfuscate but to cushion and support. She has wanted to communicate in plain, simple language, free of jargon; each of her words of significant weight and substance, like the shining river pebbles in the children's sieve on the day they panned for gold. But she no longer has the capacity to choose her words carefully. Her mind is clogged, silted up. The words are slow in coming and, when they come, are reduced, almost hollow. And around them, between them, leak the words she never meant to say. It is not that she says what she is thinking: candour, at least, would be something. Instead there is a listlessness, a lack of discrimination, so that the word *doctor* coming from her mouth might just as well be followed by the word *fraud*.

She thinks always of herself. How she hates herself for it. Her life is now lived in the confines of her skull. What sort of life is that? She had thought that once she became a doctor she would abandon narcissism for good, and for a long time her patients were enough. To spend a whole day in the service of others: what freedom from self. She can no longer do it. After one or two patients she must now yield to her own demands: *Give me water! Let me rest!*

Maybe it is a cause she needs; something larger and more significant than her own whining concerns. Climate change, the logging of old growth forests: here are things worth thinking about, worth crying over. In the Styx Valley of Tasmania, deep within a forest of ancient eucalypts, she should chain herself to the trunk of a giant swamp gum and there, on the soft forest floor she will lie, looking up through the canopy, fixing the sky, as the bulldozers roll towards her.

First, the local anaesthetic. The circular path of the needle; through gum then cheek then hard palate; the crescendo sting; the hard, angry thumping of her heart as the adrenaline bites. The periodontist lifts the scalpel from the tray. The incision in her gum is as a tongue's lick but she finds herself shaking nevertheless: *shaking like a leaf*, a half-withered leaf, *in the autumn of her years*, about to fall from the branch. *Pride comes before a fall. She who falls from a height falls hardest.*

'Yes,' the periodontist says eventually. 'Two fractures through one of the roots.' *Not one, but two!* 'Look at that,' he says to his nurse, who then bends forward over her open mouth. *Twenty cents a look*. 'I will have to remove it.'

Is it too late to go back? If this were a dream (*Wake up, it's only a dream!*) she could wind the years back, back, back—so many years now—to that first day she sat in Doctor Leonard's chair, in that bright, white room and—*Zing!*—his dental probe is a magic wand and, as he touches her teeth, one by one, they become perfect, whole, impermeable to future assaults, and her gums, too, are pink, scalloped, translucent. *And while you're at it, dear Doctor L—Zing!*—and her skin is silken, creamy, dewy—*Throw away your lotions and potions, you no longer need them!*—and she arises from the dentist's chair glowing and serene. *But wait! There's more!*—her hand on her belly, where inside a baby grows instead of a stone.

The periodontist has the tooth in the pliers' grip. She feels the rocking movement of tooth against bone as a creaking sound deep within her ear—*near and yet so far*. 'Long roots,' the periodontist mutters to his nurse. There is sweat on his forehead.

She grips the arms of the chair. *Hold onto your seats, ladies and gentlemen. We're in for a rough ride.* He pulls hard and she feels the resistance of tooth and jaw, body and soul. *Fight, fight on!* Then, suddenly: *Give up, the fight is over.* All at once, she has a sense of something giving way, something irreplaceable, a footfall closer to death. The periodontist's eyes smile above his mask. 'Would you like to take it home?' he asks.

Blood trickles down the back of her throat and, in the hole in her jaw where a tooth once was, a blood clot has started to form.

May 27

The sun is shining on the water. She should not be here: she has work to do. The water is glinting with silver light, gold light. It is not enough to say the water is smooth: it is glossy, lacquered, as if — from her position on the sand — she could bend down, run her hand over its surface and feel the unyielding coolness of polished stone. Today the ships are on the move. The largest ship, laden with containers, leads the way and the others follow, trailing across the horizon, towards the port. They travel in an orderly line, a decorated procession, the saddled beasts of the sea, bearing gifts. She imagines the sailors on board, their blood stirring as the ships' engines start anew and the wind — sea breeze, salt air — rises once more against their faces. Do they still feel the wind against their faces or are they grown so used to it that they only now feel the absence of wind as an abnormal closeness, a claustrophobia?

Where to, now? The cargo unloaded, their ship might again turn for home. She imagines where home could be: a grimy port town or a small fishing village on some sparkling sea, where women wear patterned headscarves and men play backgammon in the brightly painted bars at the water's edge. Is home remembered with fondness? Or only as the absence of movement, a sense of things closing in?

Is she not sorry? Is that the problem? That there is a problem is not in doubt. But as to the root of it, the heart of it. To get to the heart of the problem: this is what is required. As to the difficulty of this, this journey to the heart, she is not so sure. Once she would have thought it both difficult and dangerous but, in these brave times of minimally invasive cardiology, the heart is no longer inaccessible, no longer a secret place. To access the heart, one would once have needed to cut open the chest with a vertical incision, and split the breastbone to expose the beating organ beneath. But there are now alternative routes; more circuitous, one might say more devious, but with far less resultant morbidity. The pain of coronary artery disease can now be alleviated—with the patient awake—by a balloon on the end of a catheter threaded from groin to heart, the catheter snaking its way along the aorta and into the narrowed coronary arteries, against the direction of blood flow. An atrial septal defect, a hole in the heart, can be patched in the same manner. The heart, no longer seen with the naked eye, has become more accessible, less mysterious. But she must not let technology distract her from her purpose. To delve deep, to find the heart of the problem, technology is not required: she requires only what is already in her head.

As a doctor it has been her role, her life's work, to solve the problems of others. In fifteen minutes she is able to identify and solve a patient's problem, or at the very least identify the steps that need to be taken towards achieving a solution. She has learned to name a problem, to stare it down, to pull it apart and reframe it, rebuild it so that the reconfiguration of its parts now constitutes a solution—like the rapid reworking of a Rubik's cube, the flip side of the problem becomes the solution. There is nothing to be afraid of. She must do as she tells her patients in cognitive therapy: strip back the negative emotions—anger, sadness, shame, fear, guilt—so that the real problem, the twisted thinking that underlies these emotions, is exposed for what it is: irrational and destructive. The guilt she feels, the guilt that eats away at her insides: isn't this guilt simply a consequence of her irrational belief that she *should* never err, that she *must* be perfect? Rid yourself of *shoulds* and *musts*, she urges her patients: she is an evangelist of sorts. Her guilt in itself is nothing of substance—even though it gnaws at her from inside, it is nothing of substance: it is the belief in infallibility that weighs her down. If she can exorcise this belief, she has solved the problem.

But even as she strives for rationality, the ground gives way beneath her, and her heart lurches—the heart again, always it comes back to the heart—as if she has dropped from a height, dropped into a chute, plunged into darkness and finds herself descending rapidly, as if inside a water slide, in the dark, with the water rushing down alongside her, there is nothing to impede her descent: she must go down until the end with nothing to hold onto, until she again finds herself floundering in self-doubt and flooded with despair.

Is it that *her* heart is too weak or too stony? Is it that the heart of the problem is her imperfect, unrepentant heart?

May 28

At nine o'clock she enters the foyer of the County Court and takes a seat to wait for John. He arrives soon after, deep in conversation with another man, whom she recognises as Fergus Gray, the barrister she once met at John's office. John had told her Fergus would be here today. 'Just to add a little more weight to our case,' he had said with a wry smile and she had felt insubstantial, hollow.

John eventually sees her, sitting in her corner, and ushers over his companion. She stands to meet them and Fergus shakes her hand. His grip is warm and meaty and she is embarrassed by how cold and dry her hand must feel in his. Fergus's face, too, is fleshy, his cheeks laced with fine red capillaries, perhaps the beginnings of rosacea. He reminds her, despite his dark pinstripes and shiny shoes, of a farmer—a wealthy farmer of the Western District, with his high colouring, sandy hair and earthy, broad stance. A product of generations of good breeding and a diet of country air, red meat and fresh cream. John guides her to the elevator and they enter. Once inside she stands between them. They are her bodyguards now.

John presses the button for the third floor.

'Remind me, John. Who's acting for the plaintiff?' Fergus asks, over her head. John names the solicitor. Fergus sniffs. 'She's a real bleeding heart. We'll have to keep her in check, or she'll have the mediator in tears.'

The lift doors slide open onto an empty corridor. John and Fergus both hold back, waiting for her to exit first. She walks in front of them, sick with treachery. *A bleeding heart.* She is reminded of a picture from her childhood, a picture that hung in the spare bedroom of her grandparents' house, of a beatific Jesus, his heart exposed in his chest, surrounded by light. A crown of thorns encircled his heart and, where a thorn had pierced its flesh, a drop of blood flowed or, rather, was held suspended. When staying in that room on visits to her grandparents she would wake during the night to the sound of cars on the nearby highway. Lying in her bed, Sophie asleep across the room, she would watch the arc of headlights through the gaps in the blinds as, for an instant, they illuminated the picture of Jesus, his sorrowful, forgiving eyes alighting briefly upon her. She had thought a bleeding heart to be a sign of compassion. She, too, has been moved by the stories her patients have told her over the years; moved, yes, to tears, shed in private moments between appointments or in the car on the way home from work. The stories she has heard: one would have had to be a monster not to cry. And now, here she stands, side by side with these two men who deplore tears, who see them as a sign of weakness or, worse, as a manipulative trick. Her lawyers, her advocates, these two men of the establishment, decrying the bleeding heart, their own hearts bloodless and stony. They are working in this way for her. What, then, has she become?

There is no time to ponder this. John has opened the door to a room and is bidding her enter. From the corridor she sees blue-striped carpet, an oval table and chairs, and, against the wall, a pair of crutches.

Afterwards, in the lift, John offers to call her a taxi, taking his phone from his pocket as proof of his intentions. She declines his offer. She has organised the boys each to go to a friend's house after school. She is not wanted at home, not yet. Besides, she does not want to return to an empty house. 'I'll walk to the train station,' she tells him.

'If you're sure,' he says, frowning.

Perhaps he is unused to his clients catching trains home from court. Either that, or he fears she is about to throw herself under one. Does he have children? She has never asked him. Strange, after three years, how little they know of each other. If, when all this is over, she were by chance to see him somewhere, she would turn her head, lower her eyes and pass him as she would a stranger. No, more than that. She would step out in front of moving traffic to avoid him; this man who, again and again, has reduced her, not to tears—he has *not* made her cry, she will not give him the satisfaction; instead, with his incessant questions—questions as dry as the paper on which they are written—he has whittled her down, reduced her to nothing more than the sum of her mistakes. Today, then, has been her day of reckoning, when her mistakes have been tallied and given a price.

Three hours in that windowless room. Only a table's width between her and the boy: so close her extended hand might have met his across the table. So close he could have struck her over the head with one of his crutches, or pushed its stoppered end hard into her chest so that she toppled backwards in her chair. Instead they had both sat with folded arms, staring at the stripes in the carpet until their eyes watered. At least, that is her excuse for her smarting eyes; she cannot speak for him.

She glances at John, who is looking at the floor, his phone to his ear. The message to which he listens with such concentration might be from a client; someone just like her. She is too hard on him. If not John at her side these last three years, it would have been another; one, perhaps, with a colder heart. It is not John's fault, any of it. *Delayed diagnosis of a life-threatening disease.* An X-ray—such a simple test, so easily arranged—*yet she did nothing.* The fault is hers alone.

The lift doors open and John ushers her across the foyer and out onto the street, where everyone, it seems, is going about their daily lives without interruption. John begins to speak, but she shakes her head to silence him.

'Please, let's not discuss it. I don't think I can go over it now.'

'I understand. His mother must have rattled you. It's unfortunate she was there.'

She imagines his mother's thin hands locked around her neck, shaking her with such ferocity that her brain knocks against her skull. Yes, she is rattled: her brain and body shaken to the core by what she has seen and heard. *Three whole hours.* Was she sick, his mother? Not just distressed, but sick—a fever, perhaps—something that explained her brittleness, her agitation, that restless movement of her thin, dry hands. She had glanced up, just once, to see his mother's eyes fixed upon her. Such a look! No pretence, no obfuscation. *That is what it is like to be hated.*

To John she only says: 'She came to support her son. You can't blame her for that. Whether or not she was there, it was always going to be difficult.'

'Difficult, yes, but not insurmountable. Remember, we have made an offer of compromise; a good and fair offer. I'm reasonably confident they will accept it.'

'When will you know?'

'The offer stands for a fortnight. They will get back to us with an answer before then.'

She leaves John at the court steps and walks south along William Street. It is not an area of the city she knows well, this enclave of court precincts and legal chambers, but maybe she should search out its hiding places—the narrowest laneways, the most dimly lit bars—in case one day she needs to return. Will it all end today, as John predicts? Or will she continue to wait—months and months of waiting—for another day like this? No, worse than this, a hundred times worse.

Two barristers stand at the kerb in front of her, the hems of their black-winged gowns lifting in the wind, two stiff, white wigs perched upon their greying heads.

Two magpies, hovering, ready to swoop. If they could they would pluck out her eyes. An eye for a limb; is that how it should be? *Do it, then, and get it over with.*

She will not think of it. She will not remember what was said ... The sound of the boy's sob, the only sound he made all morning ... a single violent sob, torn from his throat during his counsel's opening words. She had remembered him as softer, sweeter looking, but today, across the table, his face had lengthened, grown sharp and his chest seemed sunken. It could have been the way he was sitting—slouched back in his chair, his head down—that gave him that sunken, defeated air. She had not seen his legs under the table, she had been spared that ... But had she taken away his chance of beauty? Had she done that, too?

At the corner of William and Collins streets, a young man sits cross-legged on the pavement, head bowed, clutching a cardboard sign. *Due to my disability I am unable to work. Please help me buy food.* There is dirt under his fingernails, dirt ground into the fine lines of his hands. She could put a fifty-dollar note into his upturned cap, but how would that change anything? Nothing she can do will make the slightest difference.

She turns into Collins Street and heads eastward, over Swanston Street and up the hill. She passes the antiquarian bookshop and the Athenaeum Theatre, the paint peeling on its Corinthian columns. The message board outside the Scots' Church reads: *Every Sunday at 5.30 pm. Join us for scripture readings in a contemporary setting. Find God again and repent!*

As a child, repentance had been a fortnightly act. *Bless me, Father, for I have sinned.* She would leave the confessional and pray for redemption, her bare knees cold against the hard kneeling board. Such repentance, so easily conjured, so lightly carried! Even as a child she knew her prayers were whispered, not in sorrow for her wrongdoings, but to insure herself against the consequences of sin. Was there nothing in her heart, not even then? At fifteen she was at last able to reject it all on scientific grounds: Darwinism, humanism, the shining light of medical endeavour. *Not a priest, but a doctor.* But science, it seems, has let her down: no, rather it is she who has disgraced science; the scientific principles of observation and deduction, cause and effect.

At the Paris end of Collins Street she hears the town-hall clock chime the hour: one, two, three o'clock. Already the daylight is waning. Has she really been wandering all this time? The wind has dropped and a fine mist has gathered, hovering in the branches of the bare plane trees, threatening to descend. From the dark interior of the basement café at her feet come the sounds of plates being stacked, the *hiss* of the espresso machine. She has not eaten since breakfast but the smells of coffee and frying onions turn her stomach.

In the ground-floor window of the clothing boutique above, an old brass lamp stands on a polished table, shedding soft, seductive light onto the pavement. *Soldes! Sale!* is painted across the window in elegant red letters. She could buy a dress for this evening. Should she go inside and browse those sparsely hung racks, then, her arms casually draped with silk and cashmere, slip behind the brocade curtain? Is it a question of daring or simply a matter of money? To spend a thousand dollars on a single dress. The sheer depravity of it! Sometimes she longs to throw caution to the wind. The heaviness of principle has made her sour and bony. A thousand-dollar dress would not be enough to hide her defects. She lingers on the pavement while, in the lamplight, behind the brocade curtain, the clothes slip from her arms and fall to the floor in a soft, voluptuous pile.

She is back at home, cooking pasta for the boys when Paul telephones.

'How did it go?'

He asks out of obligation: she can hear it in his voice. He does not really want to know. 'I can't talk now,' she replies. 'I will tell you later.' She, too, will keep up the pretence, although she already knows that the time for telling has passed. She will never tell him. Never. He will not ask again.

'I've been caught up in a meeting. I won't have time to come home before the dinner. I'm sorry. Can you get there by yourself?'

She can hear the buzz of conversation in the background. A woman laughs, and she feels as if she is the butt of an elaborate, malicious joke.

'Won't you need to change?' she asks. Beneath the hiss of boiling water, the clanging of the saucepan lid, her voice trembles.

'I've brought some clothes to work with me. I'll see you there, around seven-thirty.'

He is not coming home. On this day of all days, he is not coming home. She has her out, and yet now, when it has been handed to her on a platter, she finds she does not want to take it. While the boys are eating dinner, she goes to her wardrobe and hunts until she finds a black knee-length skirt and a beaded top. She holds the shirt to her nose: it smells faintly of deodorant and fried food, of having lain fallow in the wardrobe since last year's awards dinner. She searches on the floor of the wardrobe for some shoes. What did she wear last year? She has never liked the idea of evening shoes: a lot of money for such silly, flimsy things, so bad for one's feet. Trying them on, teetering in front of shop mirrors makes her feel foolish. Besides, she has always thought her ankles and calves too thick to wear fine-heeled shoes. Her black summer sandals, with their sensible block heels, will have to do. She will wear them with pantyhose, as her legs are white and unshaven and her toenails unpainted. The big toenail on her left foot is thickening a little at the base: it is possible she has the beginnings of a fungal infection. *This is who I am*, she thinks. *This is who I have become.*

What is she doing? Here she stands, clothes hangers in hand, taking stock of her shoes, her unshaven legs when today ... No, she will not think about it. She dresses quickly, looks at herself in the mirror. The skirt feels tight around her waist and pulls across her stomach, emphasising its fullness. She sees she has developed a little round paunch. She will have to undo the skirt button. Elsewhere, it seems she has lost weight: her collarbones protrude from the scooped neckline and the tendons in her neck stand out, sharp and strained. She will wear a necklace, something substantial, or a scarf tied jauntily around her throat, as other middle-aged women do. The combination of sandals and black pantyhose is frumpy, ridiculous. She has never been much interested in fashion, although there was a time—surely not so long ago?—when aesthetics mattered. The pantyhose and open-toed shoes are simply not aesthetic, she can see that. And she, an architect's wife! She has not lived up to expectations. No matter. It does not matter now.

The doorbell rings: it must be the babysitter. She crosses the room to the window and peers through a gap in the curtains. It is Deirdre. The boys will not be happy to see her: they say she has a short temper and does not let them read in bed. Poor Deirdre, always last choice on the agency list yet, despite her pursed lips and her bedtime rules, not without tenderness. A dutiful daughter, still living with her mother; a chronic invalid, confined to her bed. An invalid and a tyrant, too, if the truth be told. She knows all this: it is her job to ask questions. Where are her lipsticks? She finds one hidden behind a photo frame: the lid has been squashed down and the lipstick tip is broken. She will speak to Joe about it. No, it does not matter. She understands that Deirdre—despite her sour expression, her trashy women's magazines—asks for kindness and inclusion, wants to be part of something outside of her favourite television programs and her mother's complaints: but how to explain this to the boys, who find her only mean-spirited? On her children's behalf she must set aside Deirdre's needs and firmly negotiate a reasonable bedtime. Or should she be teaching the boys to be more compassionate? Are they old enough to understand such things? Does she have anything in the pantry for supper? Deirdre will be peeved if the supper plate is not left in its usual place, covered with plastic wrap, the matching cup and saucer alongside. The kitchen is still dirty: she must find the time to at least wipe down the benches before she leaves. *Always a string of useless imperatives. I have let such things take over. What has happened to beauty and love? I have let them slip away.* The doorbell rings again and, sensing Deirdre's mounting displeasure, she hurries to the door.

On the way, in the back of the taxi, she begins to bleed. She searches her bag and finds, in a side pocket, a single tampon, its cellophane wrapping starting to come away at one end. She puts it inside the pocket of her coat. It is warm in the taxi and, as the driver has shown no desire to talk, it is blessedly quiet. She could spend the whole night like this, cocooned in her velour-lined cabin, gliding through the city streets. *Take me to Sydney!* she might say and her silent driver would carry her northwards while she slept, lulled by the hum of the engine, the promise of something new and bright when she woke.

Along St Kilda Road, the branches of the elms are lit up with fairy lights. She remembers reading—years ago, in a gardening magazine she once subscribed to—about

Dutch elm disease: a fungal infection, she recalls, that had devastated the elm forests of England and Europe. It had not yet come to Australia, said the article: but be warned, be vigilant! So much disease, so many possibilities for damage and loss. She finds herself crying, perhaps anticipating the death of the trees, perhaps not. She no longer knows why she cries. Is it too late to turn around and go back?

At the National Gallery she pays the driver. She hurries through the gallery entrance to the nearest bathroom where, in the toilet cubicle, she examines the back of her skirt for telltale signs. No, she has escaped, at least for now. She smooths her skirt, reapplies lipstick. In the yellow fluorescent light her skin looks dry and sallow and the lines around her mouth extend down to her chin. Marionette lines, the cosmetic surgeons call them. In the ugly light she opens and closes her mouth in the mirror, making her jaw drop like a ventriloquist's dummy. She bares her teeth, looking for the hole where, until two days ago, a tooth resided. Yes, it is there, mocking her.

The gallery foyer is empty, save for herself and two security guards who stand, across the foyer, at the entrance to the great hall. They watch her as she walks towards them, listening, it seems, to the foolish clicking of her sandals as she crosses the hard slate floor. On she goes, *clickety-clack*, past the water wall, where as a child she would put her hands to the glass, holding them there as the water—real water, cold and clear—trickled over her widespread fingers. To be that child again or, better still, a different child: one who knew her limitations and never exceeded them.

The security guards, identically posed with legs apart and hands clasped behind their backs, regard her coolly—is there the flash of a look exchanged between them? Having seen so many well-dressed guests enter these doors, have they grown contemptuous of those in more shabby attire? For a moment she thinks they will refuse her entry. *My husband is inside*, she will have to explain. *He is nominated for an award. I, however, rather than being rewarded, am being punished for an act of negligence. Strange, is it not, that a husband and wife can find themselves in such different situations?*

But, luckily, she is saved her little speech: the shorter man swings open the heavy door and, with a nod of his shaven head, bids her enter. Her breathing quickens as she anticipates the scene: the conversation dwindling to an icy silence as all faces in the hall—the women, red-lipped, in crisp geometric shirts, the men in well-cut black—turn to look her up and down. *Cinderella at the ball*, they will whisper to each other behind manicured hands. *But the sad woman has subverted the fairytale, having come in her workaday rags and her open-toed shoes, her face smeared with kitchen grime*. She waits, the door closing silently behind her, but the conversation in the hall gives no hint of flagging and no one looks her way. Above her the stained-glass ceiling gleams, a jagged, crude patchwork of colour: cobalt blue, emerald green, the seething red of fresh menstrual blood. She once read that the artist who designed the ceiling took five whole years to cut the thick sheets of glass, fitting one piece against another on the dusty floor of his studio. Every day his hands would be cut by the splinters that flew from his grinding blade, by the unforgiving edges of his cruel glass jigsaw as he lifted and coaxed each piece into place. Five years with blood on his hands.

A heavy, dragging band of pain encircles her pelvis, radiating down her thighs. If she were of a different culture or time she might be forbidden to enter this temple of art—this place of secular worship with its religious glass ceiling—during menstruation. But here, in Melbourne, in the early part of the twenty-first century, the rules are not so clear. It might be easier if they were. She feels unclean, unworthy enough. What has she to do with art and beauty? Her work is with the sick and damaged. People speak of the art of medicine, but her work has nothing to do with aesthetics: if there is art to be found in treating the sick, it is of an inferior form. She stands against the wall—*a little mouse*—her black clothes somehow a lesser shade of black than those around her, her body bleeding for less than an hour and, yet, already drained. Is there another woman here tonight who feels as she does: stooped and crushed, exhausted with the effort of pretending that everything is as it was, when, in fact, the opposite is true? She has grown so used to pretending, she scarcely knows how to be herself any longer. Or is it that the self that was is splintered, irredeemable?

In the faces around her she recognises Paul's partner, Dominic. He is talking to another couple she also recognises: a husband and wife, both architects, with whom she has been to dinner once or twice, the last time being a few weeks after the writ had been served. She does not remember much of that evening, at an Italian restaurant in one of the city's more fashionable lanes, save that, during the dinner, around the time the main course was served, she had decided never to dine with architects again. It was not just that the three of them, Paul and the married couple, whose names have escaped her now—she had better not catch their eye—talked architecture for most of the evening. She had never much minded this before. It was more the sudden terror that descended on her in that place as, leaning back against the upholstered banquette while the waiter placed steaming plates of pasta before them and Paul and the couple talked on and on, she wished with all her heart for the restaurant floor to open up and swallow her into oblivion. Since that evening the terror has descended many times, so she now knows that architects are not particularly to blame.

She begins to make her way through the crowd, skirting the clusters of guests, catching fragments of conversation that come to her, coded like a foreign language. The mood in the hall is enthusiastic, intense. Such enthusiasm! She cannot begin to understand it. Tomorrow they will still talk of tonight; rehashing the evening's events at the office espresso machine, lingering at each other's desks to praise or malign award winners and speech makers, while she will be shut in her consulting room, alone with her thoughts: alone, despite her patients, for she cannot share her thoughts with them. Her patients will divulge their secrets, to be kept safe by her, whereas she can tell them nothing. *My husband is having an affair with a younger woman, a pretty young woman.* If she were to tell, that is what she might say. *My husband is entranced by—perhaps even loves— a young woman with an anklet of silver leaves; a woman who knows how to make men happy. It is something I have not been taught. Or have failed to learn.* The loneliness of her work! Sometimes her thoughts threaten to engulf her. If she worked in an architect's office, flooded with natural light, surrounded by fine drawings, the hum of ideas, could she escape her thoughts? She, too, would go to meetings, would sit at an oval table with people on every side and become transparent in the sunlight, her only substance the reflections of the visions of others. Her mind would become a stockpile of beautiful things, tangible things: sparkling glass upon soft-grained timbers upon girders of shining steel. Weightless and incandescent, she would reach towards the sky and laugh.

She sees Paul, seated at a table near the front of the hall. Beside him sits Kate, fair-haired, bare-shouldered, in a silky green dress that shimmers and glows, finding and holding the light reflected from the glass ceiling. Or is it the light from a thousand admiring eyes that ignites her from within? Such a rich, emerald green, her dress: it is opaque Belgian glass, green amber, cat's-eye; greedily holding the light so that, around her, all is cast in shadow. No black for lovely Kate; Kate of the emerald green and burnished gold; of warm sun and fresh, sweet, waving grass; patriotic in her beauty; green-and-gold Kate of summer's ripeness. Paul leans towards her, deep in conversation. Standing in the shadows, crumpled and grey, she is close enough to see their mouths moving, their lips parting in smiles and, through their parted lips, the tips of their tongues that dance back and forth. If she were to move a little closer could she see into their hearts? Paul wears his black suit. She knows it well enough—the waistband that had to be taken in, the faint stain on the left sleeve of the jacket the cleaners could not remove—but his pale green shirt she cannot place. He has never worn green before, maybe because she has never thought to suggest it. Her talent has never been for colour and contour. She has bandaged his sprained ankle, administered to his headaches: her skills have been of a more plain and practical nature.

He has not yet seen her. She can watch a little longer, watch until Kate reaches out to straighten his collar, to touch his face, her fingernails red like blood. Then, as the master of ceremonies walks to the dais and a hush descends over the hall, it will be time to leave, pushing through the crowd, resisting Dominic's restraining arm, kicking off her ugly shoes and running in her ugly stockinged feet, wailing in pain as she flees the scene: an impostor, a banshee, a black-hearted witch.

The boys are still awake when she gets home. They run down the hall to greet her and she holds them to her, one in each arm. Deirdre follows, frowning. She pleads a migraine and pays the babysitter a whole night's fee.

'You don't look well,' Deirdre tells her, shaking her

head of stiff, grey hair.

Is it sympathy she sees in Deirdre's eyes? She has an urge to tell her the truth—but where to begin? It would be too much for Deirdre, who has never known the balancing act of marriage, the ebb and flow, the subtle shifts and realignments, the failures. And she would have to tell the whole truth. *Paul is in love with a pretty young woman.* Because? *Because I have failed to give him what he wants. He is a good man. He would not fall in love unprovoked.* The cramps in her pelvis are so vice-like she can barely stand.

She sees Deirdre to the door, a boy on each side. 'Come here,' she says, squeezing them to her, feeling the hardness of their skulls against her ribs. They are hard-headed boys. They belong to her. 'Time for bed. Dad will be home soon.'

Paul, Paul, Paul, Paul, Paul. Saying his name will not return him to her. Who is she, now he is gone? For half her life he has been with her in thought and word, in reflection and shadow. To see herself she has always looked to him. She would not care if his absence was only physical: an empty chair at the dinner table, a cold patch in the bed, so long as she could see in his face or hear in his voice—brittle with anger, thickened with disgust—that something remained: a core, a kernel, something to grasp. But this: this absence of attachment, this slippage of caring. That he is no longer with her, in love or in hate—how will she bear it? There is no yawning chasm inside her where once he resided; instead, in every cell of her body, an impoverishment of substance, a depletion of self.

May 29

In the morning she is ready to leave the house with the boys before Paul is awake. At the bedroom door she stops. 'Listen to Dad snoring,' she urges them. 'See? He's there, still asleep.'

'Why wouldn't he be there?' William asks. He is watching her closely.

'I just wanted you to know he got home safely,' is all she can think of to say.

After dropping the boys at school, she drives to the foreshore and parks the car where once she saw her vision: the strange aquatic creature that had leaped above the waves one evening at dusk. But today the water is grey and choppy and the sand is littered with plastic. The seagulls, buffeted by the wind, screech in ugly protest at the state of the world.

She shares the car park with three other cars. Who are they, these other people who, on this grey, cold morning, sit alone in their cars, staring out to sea? She would like to think their intentions are benign—a brisk walk along the beach, a breakfast stop—but instead she reads desperation and suffocating loneliness.

She is twenty minutes late to work. Margaret meets her in the corridor. 'I'll get you a cup of tea,' Margaret says. 'I've asked your first patient to reschedule and I've blocked off a few appointments through the day.'

She nods and tries to smile. Dear Margaret, always so kind. Kind to the end: so kind she will not ask any questions. She cannot speak for fear of what she will say. *Take me home with you, dear Margaret, and wrap me in a blanket, one that you have knitted in soft, white wool, as fine as babies' hair. Feed me tea so sweet you could stand a spoon in it, and toast dripping with honey. Keep me warm. Let me fade away.*

The day moves at a snail's pace. She often looks at the clock, fearing time has stood still and she will be fixed at her desk forever. Above all else she wants to be home; home with her boys, the doors locked and the curtains drawn. Her boys, her lifeblood. *Let nothing happen to my boys.*

Dreading an interrogation from David or Rohan, she escapes the clinic at lunchtime and wanders through the local shopping strip. As she passes by her regular café, she notices a couple, sitting at a window table. At first glance an unremarkable pair; neither attractive nor young nor, to all appearances, wealthy. Yet they are happy: she sees that immediately. It is not just that they are holding hands across the table. Everything about them speaks of happiness; an aura of contentment and love that radiates through the windowpane and touches her heart.

Perhaps Paul is—this very moment—having lunch with Kate. They, too, are sitting at the window of a café near their office. No, they are in some warm, shadowy corner, laughing softly, making plans ... She closes her eyes until the image fades. She cannot think about it. She does not have the strength.

Another patient—her second last for the day—has just left the room and she is writing a few hasty notes when she becomes aware of someone standing in the doorway. She looks up to see a woman in a heavy woollen coat and dark sunglasses, clutching a handbag. It is the handbag that most fixes her attention: a bright pink bag appliquéd with red hearts. It does not fit with the woman who stands there as if in a trance, her hair dishevelled and streaked with grey. The face she somehow knows yet cannot place: the sunglasses seem to hide so much. She must be a patient. No, the context is wrong. All this passes through her mind in an instant and, even as she bends forward and pushes her feet against the floor, even as her body attempts instinctively to stand, there is still no spark of recognition. The woman enters the room, closes the door behind her and removes her glasses. It is Ben's mother.

Her first reaction is to step backwards, away from

the desk. She feels the tensing of her muscles and the quickening of her pulse, but she is also dimly aware that her body's response is not one of shock. As Virginia Feltham stares at her from across the room, her handbag gripped tightly to her chest, there is, held deep within that charged and dangerous moment, a sense of things falling gently, inevitably into place; a sense that something has come full circle. She had thought her day of reckoning had come and gone. Not so, it seems. Is her real trial to take place here and now, in this ordinary room? *Guilty as charged. I offer no defence.* She shakes from head to foot with fear. She feels, too, an overwhelming tiredness; a lethargy so deep that she could, this very minute, crumple to the floor and sleep for a hundred years.

Ben's mother stands against the wall, still hugging the pink handbag. She has not yet spoken. There is no need. The woman is disturbed, deeply so: she sees that now. But the time for diagnoses and soothing words has passed. It is too late for the examination couch, the prescription pad. Could it be that, all along, Virginia Feltham has needed a doctor, not a lawyer? The irony of it, yet she cannot raise a smile. She is so, so tired. Virginia fumbles with the clasp of the handbag. Does she have time to lift the phone and call Margaret? The redundancy of legal argument: all those mounds of paper, all those words. Actions, in the end, speak louder. It is a kitchen knife, a large one: a knife for cutting meat, for slicing through bone.

David is with her in the ambulance, checking the flow of the intravenous line. She feels, as if through cotton wool, a heavy bandage around her thigh and, under the bandage, a dull, diffuse ache. There had been pain, bad pain, but now it is lessened: someone must have given her morphine. With her free hand she pulls on David's shirtsleeve. 'Don't let William and Joe know what has happened,' she whispers thickly. 'Tell them it was an accident.'

'Yes, of course. I will speak to Paul.'

It occurs to her she could say something else: report on her condition or ask what intravenous solution he is giving her. But, in fact, there is nothing she needs to communicate, nothing she needs to know. The distant throbbing in her thigh is somehow comforting. *I feel pain, therefore I am alive*. It is as simple as that.

She wakes in her hospital bed at the touch of a hand on her face. It is Joe's. William stands next to him, trying not to cry. She hugs them both as best she can, despite the drip in her arm. 'I am all right,' she tells them. 'See? I am all here.' And it is true. She feels the pressure of both calves against the mattress. She moves both feet, even wriggles her toes under the sheet.

Paul stands at the foot of the bed, his hands in his pockets. How young he looks, how handsome; barely changed from when they met, so long ago now, when it had seemed so much was possible. She remembers the dinner, the award.

'Did you win?' she asks him.

'Yes, we won.'

'Congratulations.' She smiles at him. He moves towards her and kisses her on the forehead. It is relief she feels; only relief. She has not impeded him. Whatever her faults, she has not stood in his way.

'I will be home tomorrow,' she says to William and Joe as they leave. 'And hopping around on crutches.' To Paul she would like to say something, too, but this is not the time or the place. Instead she gently nods her head, hoping that in her gesture he sees something of what he seeks.

Her mother visits with a bunch of orange tulips, and cannot rest until she has found a vase. Once the flowers are neatly arranged she takes a seat next to the bed.

'You should have an emergency alarm in your surgery,' she says briskly, then her voice falters. 'Anna, I'm so worried about you.'

Free of foundation and lipstick, her mother's face is pale and the lines on her forehead and cheeks seem more deeply etched. *Those are my lines*, she thinks. *That is the face I will one day have*. A woman's face marked by hard work and love: an honourable ageing. It is not such a terrible thing, after all. She thinks back to the evening of her father's death, when her mother had phoned her to come. She had gone into the garden where he still lay, the old mower keeping vigil, his body strewn with flowers that had fallen from the jacaranda tree. She knelt by his side and put her fingers to his neck, as was her duty, while her mother stood behind her, crying quietly. They had sat for a while on the verandah steps, just the two of them. Then, when it was dark, they had gone inside to call Sophie.

She reaches for her mother's hand and holds it between hers. 'I'm going to take some time off work. It will be all right.'

The trauma surgeon tells her she was lucky. 'The knife just missed the femoral artery. You've had a decent rip through part of your quadriceps muscle. We've debrided the wound and cauterised a few small blood vessels, but otherwise things are pretty much intact. An unusual site for a stabbing,' he adds. 'Most stab wounds are to the upper body.'

When next she opens her eyes the ward is dark and Sophie is sitting at her bedside, reading a magazine. Seeing she is awake, Sophie bends over to kiss her.

'Sorry I'm so late,' she whispers. 'I had to wait until Rosie went to sleep.' She picks up a takeaway cup from the bedside table. 'Here, I've brought you a hot chocolate.'

She takes the drink from her sister and tentatively sips. It is lukewarm but sweet, comforting.

'God, you look awful,' Sophie says. 'Did you lose a lot of blood?'

May 30

David drops by before work. 'This is the first hospital visit I've done for a while,' he jokes. The hospital is well out of his way. She is touched that he has come. He is a good friend, a good man.

'I've spoken to your medical defence people, told them what happened. And the police, of course.'

'Police?' She struggles to sit upright. 'Surely they don't need to be involved.'

David looks surprised. 'I've reported the incident to them. Both Rohan and I felt it was the right course of action.' He perches on the edge of her bed. 'Naturally, it's up to you whether you press charges or not. But this is assault, Anna. It's a crime, in anyone's book.'

She shakes her head. 'She isn't well, David. She needs assessment, proper care.'

'Isn't that for the police and the courts to decide?' He folds his arms and regards her steadily. 'I know you think you had a part to play in this.' He gestures towards her leg under the bedclothes. 'You might even think you deserved it in some way. But it simply isn't true. She decided to instigate legal action, not you. She can't then change her mind midstream and take justice, or revenge, or whatever you want to call it, into her own hands.'

'She couldn't bear to stand by and see her son suffer. Imagine if you had been in her position—if it were your son that lost his leg. Isn't it possible you might have done the same?'

He lightly touches her arm. 'So you're trying to put yourself in her shoes? When she wouldn't do the same for you?'

She shrugs and turns away. When she looks back David is smiling at her.

'You're a good person, Anna,' he says gently.

'Why do you say that?' There are tears in her eyes.

'Because you are prepared to forgive her.'

June 3

Brendan calls her at home. 'We were all shocked to hear what happened. John sends his regards. How are you managing?'

She has been home three days: time enough to get used to crutches. Time, too, to start reading the next novel for book club, bought for her, kindly, by Bridget, as a get-well gift. She has even been able to bake a cake, sitting at the kitchen bench to stir the batter, her leg resting on a stool. 'I am managing pretty well,' she says.

'I have some good news. Are you sitting down?' He tells her the plaintiff's side has agreed to a settlement: 'in the light of recent events,' he says. 'All in all, a reasonable outcome.' He mentions a figure.

She cannot reply. She does not know what to make of it. Three years of her life. She puts her hand to her thigh where, underneath the bandages, her wound aches, just a little. A tolerable ache: a sign of healing, perhaps.

'So, this is it,' Brendan says. 'This is where it ends.'

December 5

On Friday evening, after work, she takes William and Joe for a walk along the canal to the beach. They stroll along the foreshore path, the boys occasionally jumping the sea wall onto the sand and running into the shallows. It is still light and the air is warm and heavy; imbued, it seems, with the promise of the summer ahead.

The boys stop at an ice-cream van and she lets them buy a chocolate cone: a special treat, she tells them.

William scowls at her. 'No one says *treat* anymore. It's such a gay word.'

Her first instinct is to admonish him, but she stops herself in time. Instead, she hands him the coins for his ice cream. He eyes her cautiously as she places them on his outstretched palm, aware, she can tell, that he has just escaped a lecture. Is she too hard on him? She tries to be gentle but the urge to teach him what is right sometimes makes her exigent, almost strict. He has just turned eleven. Clumsily, angrily, hardly knowing what he does, he is starting to pull away from her. There are times she feels it as a physical wrenching, as if her own flesh were being torn from the bone. But she will not let him go, not yet.

Two nights a week and every second weekend they stay with Paul in his rented apartment. When they are away from her she worries they will not shower or clean their teeth. She worries, too, that one Sunday evening, when Paul brings them back, she will open the door to changelings, her real boys stolen and two strangers in their place. A silly fear that toys with her only when she is alone, cooking her one-woman dinner or reading in bed, the house silent save for the creaking of the floorboards, the ticking of the hallway clock. She will soon grow out of it, this fear, just as she has grown used to the absence of other things: the sound of Paul's key in the lock, his warmth in the bed.

Look at them now, standing together, William's hand resting idly on Joe's shoulder, watching the ice-cream vendor as he dips a laden cone into melted chocolate and rolls it in coloured sprinkles. They are still hers, and will always be: William, whom she must protect; and Joe, who will protect her.

As the boys eat their ice creams she watches the passers-by: older couples with small dogs; women in tracksuit pants and baseball caps, walking briskly in pairs; young couples who stroll along the sand, barefoot, holding hands. She realises that she does not simply observe these people as they pass: instead she goes further, using what she observes to classify them according to age, social status, level of education. She is even prepared to hazard a guess at their values and aspirations, these people who pass her unsuspectingly, looking out to sea or talking to their companions, unaware of her gaze. The physical characteristics of the older ones help her a little—the gait of the arthritic, the breathy wheeze of the emphysematous smoker, the plethoric face and evasive eyes of the heavy drinker—but she does not confine her observations to the medical. Why does she do this? Why sift and sort and classify and evaluate? The obvious answer is that she is a doctor and this is what doctors do. But if she had never become a doctor, would she still lean to this way of seeing the world?

William and Joe sit beside her, intent on their ice creams, licking the rim of the cone to catch the melting drops. Is it presumptuous of her to feel she knows these people's stories? Does it indicate a feeling of superiority, of omnipotence even? Doctors have been accused of these things often enough. But she does not feel powerful. At this moment, sitting here on this wall, her children beside her, Joe's thigh against hers, she feels ... What is it she feels? Not power or ambition—such things do not matter—but instead a tiny kernel of hope, a remnant of strength. She thinks of her twenty years of work, of the thousands of patients she has seen, to whom she has listened and tried to understand, tried to help as best she could. Can she lay claim to this, can she truthfully say that she did the best she could? Is this too much to claim? Is it enough? Has she observed so many people, heard so many stories that she believes she knows them all? This would suggest complacency, but that is not what she feels, sitting on this wall on this summer's evening.

If any one of these passers-by were to look at her, what would they see? A mother sitting with her children; yes, but what of her individual story? Would they read in her face the story of a woman broken by guilt and shame? Or that of a woman who can, when all is said and done, lay claim to doing the best she could?

There once was a boy ... She still tells herself this story; still sees, in her darker moments, a young man on crutches with a dog at his side. Were she now to turn her head and look back along the foreshore path, she might catch a glimpse of him, a shadow. But tonight the air is warm and still and, as she looks out across the water, her thoughts are of her children and of Christmas, coming soon. Tonight she does not feel the need to look back.

The boys have finished their ice creams and are licking the last sticky remnants from their fingers. She sends them off to the drinking fountain to wash their faces. It is still light. She looks at her watch: Paul will be arriving soon to pick them up for the weekend. Perhaps she should have left him a note, telling him where she would be. Well, let him wait. Tonight she is going to take her time. She waves to her boys, who are still at the fountain, squirting jets of water high into the air.